1 | Douglas Walter

Pantherville

---Introduction---

Over this root and that tuft of grass went the squirrel, through a narrow crevice and then amongst the bushes, some with blueberries and raspberries, some with small thorns but pretty big to the squirrel like the blade of an axe or some sort of bludgeoning instrument to a human---*Ouch*! *Ouch*! They're hard to avoid but he has tough skin; have to in a jungle.

Nuts were hidden where he'd forgotten he'd hidden them in the first place---or, second or third place. He stopped his scattershot movement---stop and go, stop and go---and sat on his haunches and breathed and wiggled his nose and whiskers, his keen sense of smell taking in so many of the jungle's and swamp's organic and seasonal odors; some of it very stinky stuff.

Nuts: He lost almost as many as he found. He couldn't smell them with all the colorful flora and primitive fauna around. Acorns aren't particularly odiferous. The strongest smell was skunk cabbage from the bog, where everything was rank; much of the rank and file in the swamp were wet, dripping and moldy, lichen and slugs everywhere, a daily example of primitive life, here and now, also around with the dinosaurs, arrived so long ago and sticking around for hundreds of millions of years, somehow surviving all that lichen and all those slugs, which have also been around a long time.

The squirrel sniffed the air and the primitive morass of life reached his nostrils, so stinky yet so alive. He didn't go near the swamp. No need: There were plenty of acorns to hoard around here and lose.

I'll just find more and hoard those, he thought. The ones he couldn't remember where they were he might find later; if much later, they'd already be very young oak trees after breaking through the earth's surface from below, Later, much later a 100-foot-tall mighty oak---with so many more acorns.

Go look for some more. He'll remember, and maybe not. That's the way of the squirrel.

The chipmunks didn't forget where they hid stuff. The squirrel wasn't sure, but the chipmunks seemed to communicate with each other better than many other creatures, even better than other small furry creatures, like moles, voles, field mice, and squirrels. They should communicate well, because they are so small.

Chipmunks tittered and twittered a lot; they had too much time on their paws, so it seemed to the squirrel, but they didn't lose track of their culinary hiding places.

Nothing bothered Butts the squirrel more than the pigeons. If the chipmunks irritated him, the pigeons enraged him. All they did was eat, crap, make babies, and sleep standing up---*if* they slept. Sharks are like that: eat, crap, make babies, (seemingly) not sleep, but the squirrel doubted there was any animal in the kingdom that shat like or as often as the pigeons.

He continued his hunt for acorns. When found and hidden again he would (again) lose track of the hiding place for a second time or even a third. Meanwhile, he kept close to the giant oak trees which plunked themselves down in the forest like erect and globular pick-up sticks, however huge, poking into the troposphere, woody and leafy sentinels, and what started pushing through the surface and meeting up with the snails and earthworms and footprints of other beasts, became enormous and, although many of the pines reached higher and closer to the clouds and harder to see their tops on foggier days, the oaks outweighed their fellow skyward-scrapers, although the conifers managed to sniff out and absorb the sun's rays from way up there and beyond the ionosphere; the seasonal rains tickled the pine needles and cones before the oaks' leaves and acorns absorbed any moisture. Photosynthesis: not much for the shrubbery and bushes.

The oaks drank the waters from inside the ground as well as any other tree in the jungle. Root-thirsty they were, gulping from below the sodden turf. Whatever the show-off pines got from first-splash victory up top, as always it wasn't a sprint but a marathon, a long-haul; one or two rain showers don't make for a champion drinker, not in the jungle.

"Let's see how well you drink up and absorb *throughout* the rainy season," the oaks said to the pines. Butts knew where the oaks were: just follow the nuts he soon lost after he hid them. He didn't need to look up and couldn't tell from the thicker roots, some of which stuck out of the ground and didn't seem to care where they went---"We don't care where we grow," said the oak roots----up and over there, right in front of him-----*Ouch! Dammit'*! He tripped over that one and ... *Crap!* ... bumped his head while trying to duck under a root doing a loop-the-loop---not even a chipmunk would've attempted to squeeze through *that*---but the squirrel in his haste to find more nuts that he'd forget again and again where he hid found out too late, bumped again and again, even forgetting where he bumped his head----*Ouch! Crap! Dammit'!!*

Panther peered through the jungle's leafy and creepy-crawly arrangement and up and down and closed his green eyes to the tree-dappling sunlight, his eyes turning yellow with the setting sun. It was an optic thing, cones giving it up to the rods. His eyes reflected the moonlight. The gator's night-eyes' glow has nothing on the panther's, whether the moon's steady glow reflected or a flickering and subtle glow with passing fireflies or a consistent if flickering beam with a distant and erupting volcano, but there were no hills around let alone mountaintops, peaks or crevasses where teutonic plates beneath could wreak surface havoc and devastation. Then again, with such sea-level terrain and swamp as was found here, flood waters were a huge---wet---pain in the ass.

They gotta' find a hole, first, thought Panther, as he glanced across to a clearing. On its borders: pine trees, shrubs, creeper vines and ash, oak and fig; some willows and a spare kapok, the creepers choking the life out of the trees they got a hold of and crept up and ... choked. But, not the pines: too spiky for the creeper.

Panther marveled once again as his best friend attempted to find acorns after misplacing the ones he'd already cached; he'd lose the ones he'd found again.

Gotta' remember where you cache. There are worse mantras. *I should send in the chipmunks to help him,* and Panther yawned with that thought, then he remembered that squirrels and chipmunks don't usually get along or, at least, don't like to share. The big cat figured *let him suffer a bit longer* and *he seems to enjoy the ritual enough---losing shit, that is--- and I'm gonna' shout* and Panther thought better of it and fell asleep and the squirrel went on suffering in his daily amnesiac-like state.

No volcanic activity and lost nuts----no eruption and all nuts accounted for. The latter won't happen again. The former, an eruption, will never happen here.

Into the clearing crept, crawled, slithered, hopped, loped, swung and flew a menagerie of beasties, some not indigenous to these parts.

Beginnings: Stowaways landed ashore on floating limbs from hurricanes past; there were escapees from labs and zoos hit by hurricanes or discarded to fend for themselves; animals are captured, imported and brought against their will, to die under duress via testing or sold as exotic pets. Humans lost interest, got bored or couldn't afford their glamorous, exotic, expensive pets and flushed them in a burlap bag or baggie---- down the porcelain, through the Fiberglas, copper and polyurethane pipes, flumed into storm drains and sewers where few survive the human waste-infused water.

Tossing from an open car window is an option.

The grounded and rotting fruit attracted so many: a cornucopia of beasts, various critters in all shapes and sizes--- flying, crawling, sliding, slithering, stomping, creeping along and hopping, too, just like before. The earth shook with their arrival---many hooves, paws, claws, wide-berths, and long tails---not quite an earthquake, certainly no volcano.

Fermentation for all and for all a good buzz.

Panther had an opened left green eye watching the proceedings, the developing scene, the clearing filling up with creatures great and small. He thought: *Save me some blueberries.* (One day, the squirrel handed Panther some blueberries and said "Try these" and the big cat did. He liked. He also likes blackberries.)

They were here, escaped from greedy zoos and circuses, some C-4 provided by a rebel animal welfare cause, or hacking the software to unlock the cages and gates and electric fences; others released because they were old and sick or injured and beyond help or hope and then managed to survive the escape and journey. Whether by hurricane, eco-terrorist, or tossed from a car or truck window, *anything* was better than such confines and abuse from handlers, scientists, and loudmouthed and stupid owners and ignorant visitors to the zoos and circuses.

Blueberries sound good. Panther grew weary on his limb in the late afternoon of a hot and humid summer day in the jungle. He slept.

Pantherville

---The Cast---

Jamie, a raccoon of female persuasion, has a home under the porch of a house in an encroaching suburban area. One day, Butts, a squirrel with a passion for acorns, apples, snickers bars and co-eds, met her while foraging for nuts. She thought he *was* (nuts), he concurred, and soon had a crush on her. Everyone knows but him. She has a crush on him, too, but acts rather nonchalant about it. Everyone knows but her. Neither will admit to liking the other. So, then, *everyone* knows, but two aren't admitting the crush.

One day, while being transported to a zoo, Panther the black panther (jaguar, really) was involved in an accident and the truck transporting him flipped and he was injured. No one was alive but him. Butts, who happen to be nearby, managed to encourage him to extricate himself (the squirrel cannot fireman-carry him ... *uh uh*) from a busted up cage that was his temporary prison, before he ended up in a permanent prison, or zoo. Now, without his consent, Panther's in charge of Pantherville, which he didn't name, either. He doesn't care. (He shouldn't.)

Chipmunk is a chipmunk who tries to show Butts how to keep track of his nuts. He doesn't. They remain friends, anyway.

Chimp is a lab escapee. One day he shows up with Emily, an Angora cat, who might've gotten bored and left her owners. No one else can claim that kind of background. It takes a kitty. (It's doubtful that Chimp was bored as a lab experiment, probably always scared shitless.) No one knows why they're with each other. But, that's O.K. They don't fight.

Peter the pigeon is the alpha to the other flying rats. So many, too many, and they fly really crooked and shit way too much. Look out.

Seysew the African elephant is very big, weighing tons. She escaped from a reserve, whether from hurricane damage or a hacker opening the computerized gate is not known.

Roberts, a huge alligator, and Robert, a huge reticulated python, sometimes hang out together and met auspiciously, as Robert wrapped around Roberts, trying to eat him. (The gator said, "Seriously?!") Then, they became best friends. Otherwise, the constrictor likes to wrap around a limb, its head sticking out levelly, ready to criticize someone or swallow; it's a constrictor thing to do. No one's gonna' tell either how to hang on to or out with or not to eat the other. The constrictor hasn't tried to swallow the gator since.

    Rachel is a giant panda and, like Emily the Angora cat, no one really knows where she comes from. She couldn't have been released down a toilet (she's way too big), and pandas are way too cute for lab experiments (sorry, Chimp … *duuude*!) and were never very interesting to watch in a zoo; however cute, they don't move much, kinda' sluggish or sloth-like. Let's go with the hurricane thing: She washed ashore on a limb. Final answer.

    William the pygmy tarsier stands 5 inches tall and weighs in about that of a plum, with a tail longer than his body but not nearly as long as a monkey's (they're so much bigger) but longer than a black jaguar's whisker. This dude *did* arrive via hurricane---*and* on a limb! You don't wanna' try it. Just ask him.

    Elaine, the red-tail hawk, pretty much keeps to herself. No one knows the range she has. Does she fly hundreds of miles in a single day? Does she eat snakes? Yes and yes. Elaine is afraid of no one, fearless, like the wolverine.

Cindy is a wolverine (and fearless), but probably doesn't travel hundreds of miles in a day, but will attend to the miles to get her next meal; a ferocious hunter.

Brian the raven and Nathaniel the crow never miss an opportunity to show up and comment and, although not nearly as irritating as the pigeons, they shouldn't be together but they are anyway and no one knows how they connected in the first place and ... Who cares?

Clams. Why? Eat them.

Ants ... numbering thousands, millions, and kinda' nasty to a picnic---not *at* a picnic, not *with*, maybe *under*, but definitely nasty *to* a picnic because they're taking stuff. It's priceless when they confront the pigeons. You'll see.

Piranha ... They have teeth and get together and hunt in a roiling toiling boiling (not really, just rhyming) ball of hurt. They are good eating. Just ask Roberts and the lizards. (You'll find out.)

Kittay, she's a real beauty; a black jaguar, just like Panther. She's got this butt ... *Poof* ... anyway, when she's around, all hail, because she has a tendency to take charge, kind of like Jamie the raccoon. Just ask Amsterdam (he's next), Roberts, Cindy, Butts, Panther, and the rest of Pantherville.

Amsterdam is a blind silverback gorilla let go into the wild after being tortured in the lab, like Chimp was. Yeah, to be a primate can really suck. Humans can really suck: After all, the other gorillas didn't experiment on the primates, people did. It certainly wasn't a squirrel like Butts or chipmunk like Chipmunk. Nope. Not even the lizards or piranha, and certainly not the clams, if they're not already consumed.

The blind silverback gorilla has a buddy, if only for survival's sake, "providing" his eyes. (As of this writing, this uncanny and powerful gorilla has been learning to provide his own eyes.) Her name is Naja, an Egyptian spitting cobra. Nasty huge snake, but not nearly as big as Robert. That's O.K., the python isn't deadly poisonous like the Egyptian spitting cobra.

Along comes Benja, a huge Bengal tiger who might weigh as much as three jaguars. His story is similar to Panther's, although he wasn't involved in a truck crash. His owner couldn't afford his exotic tastes (re: a lot of raw meat) anymore, so released him into the jungle. He's a smart kitty. Kittay discovered him alone and disconsolate, abandoned and humanized. He'll have to learn to be wild again. Thank goodness for Kittay and, eventually, Panther.

Komodo dragons are the biggest lizards on the planet. Enter: Kinle and his clan of Komodos. They cause all kinds of trouble. Fortunately, there's Amsterdam and Rachel, Roberts, Robert, Cindy, Seysew, and a trio of wild cats who can all handle themselves in a fight. The lizards' entrance: pretty scary.

Chapters

1) Rotting Fruit & Methane.

2) Irritating Species Such As Clams, Pigeons & Ants.

3) Amsterdam Meets Naja & Vice-Versa.

4) Kittay.

5) Benja.

6) Ants Vs Pigeons.

7) Komodo Gives Chase.

8) Butts Stroke Co-Eds.

9) Attack Of The Komodos, Part II: Charge Of The S**t Brigade.

10) Strike That: Lightning.

11) Convalescing Jamie & Back To The Berries & Another Campus Chase.

12) How Cheap The Rotting Fruit, Part II: Return Of The Souse.

Pantherville

--- **A Novel** ---

By Douglas Walter

Cover Art: Laura Lee Kamp

Dad, this is for you.

Chapter 1: Rotting Fruit & Methane

"I don't *think* so!!" yelled Butts.

He stared down from an oak tree branch as a menagerie of beasts settled into the clearing that was surrounded by jungle that bordered a swamp to the east that remained boggy year 'round. Beyond this swamp were a series of roadways, two-laners, and crocodiles and alligators, snakes, spiders, rodents, wolves, wild cats, foxes and coyotes, and so many of these critters had a routine of crossing these roadways, to hunt, to head back to their broods, and many became roadkill; any time of day or night, more often at night, their guts busted, burst open and spread over the pavement.

The other sides of the jungle---north, west, south---bordered a suburb, a college, and the southern edge---well, it had no edge; it was a continuation, a merging, blending, the jungle and swamp became one, indiscriminate; whatever lived there dealt with themselves and nobody bothered them (unless they were hunted); swamp to the east and south. Lots of bog.

Somewhere out there, too, was a power plant. Roberts knew, but didn't talk much about it. More human stuff.

No one dared bother the denizens of the clearing. They didn't bother each other, either. There was this black jaguar, and he kinda' looked out for them instead of eating them.

"This is *my* backyard!!" yelled the squirrel. "My domain!!"

The other beast stopped what they were doing, which was what humans might do. It's called "curiosity" or "getting irritated". Many were mid-chew or –swallow, and a few choked on chunks and slices and bits of fruit, but they got through it--- *hack* *cough* * gasp* and a few *wheeze*s---curiosity abated; definitely an irritating little bastard.

All the beasties, scores of them, gathered like they would at a watering hole, safe and unthreatened. Panther saw to that. He had help. The elephant and gator and constrictor were protectors, too. No one messed with these formidable beasts.

The squirrel's tail shook in anger from a branch on an oak on the edge of one side of the clearing. Not one animal was afraid of Butts the squirrel, and the tail-flipping made an irritating sound. He chomped through another acorn and his cheeks swelled with the effort. Unlike some other animals, he wasn't able to talk with his mouth full, a saving grace.

"Squirrel, the fruit isn't yours," said Panther. "They're the trees' and bushes'."

"What about their poop?" said Butts. "I have to smell that!"

"Since when has yours smelled like roses?"

"Mine are tiny, so therefore insignificant."

"No shit is 'insignificant', squirrel."

Seysew the African elephant, Cindy the wolverine and several other beautiful, powerful, and dangerous creatures from the swamps and jungle again glanced up from their fruits of choice. They were used to the squirrel's rants and twitching tail while delving into the fermentating smorgasbord, and they really didn't give a shit about shit, except their own.

Butts, an herbivore, was pretty damn small, but his best friend was Panther, and he wasn't small at all, so the rest of the animals gave the squirrel a dutiful attention-span or a wide berth, depending on the situation. This situation called for tact, as well, and most were quick to look back down and enjoy the fruit of their labors.

After all, this was Happy Hour in the jungle.

Panther the black jaguar didn't have to keep a dusky and yellowing eye out for trouble---too many animals, no strays---but he did anyway. It was him and what he did, his character, make-up, carriage, and he was always alert. It was a cat thing.

There were plenty of animals at the rotting-fruit soiree to keep a look-out, and too big or dangerous to worry about any unsuspected visitors---the unwelcome guests might be unsuspecting in the reaction to their unwelcomeness---and could care less about the size of the squirrel and his fecal matter.

Panther, all 250 pounds of him, needed no help with keeping an eye out for trouble, but he got the help anyway.

Butts chewed an acorn, studied the crowd, worrying at his gums and about these *intruders*---no, they were not, but squirrels tend to their territory just like other beasts; they'll twitch their tails no matter the size of the beast below. Fearless, maybe stupid, but got a friend in a huge black jaguar. Not so stupid.

He looked on and recalled his taste for apples, but there weren't enough to go around with these guys. Not that they were getting after his stash, anyway. Let them eat the fruit here and get soused. There was enough to go around---here, yes. Fine. Like, he had a choice.

He kept a personal stash back at the college campus, kept hidden near one of his favorite trees, an old oak that stood not far from the campus cafeteria. When those apples fermented, then Butts had some spiked cider bites waiting for him---and whomever he decided to share them with ... *Jamie.* ... Chipmunk ... Panther ... Roberts ... *No* ... Seysew ... *Maybe.*

He wouldn't be able to scamper a straight line for days after consuming one of those spiked apples, but neither would anyone else---Jamie, Chipmunk or Panther. *Ooooh*, Rachel, she's a cutie. She can have some.

Amongst the besotted in the clearing was Roberts the alligator and Robert the reticulated python, two friends who met the hard way: by trying to eat each other. One day, after the 25-foot constrictor tried to choke the life out of the 20-foot gator, and the dinosaur lumbered ahead however slowly despite the snake's tremendous weight and wrap around him, they decided neither could be destroyed and became pals, which is what you do when you have no other choice.

Also bombed on fermented fructose was a massive contingent of pigeons, hundreds, maybe thousands, and they ate the rotting berries and walked and flew and perched in such a clumsy way and more than usual and that was pretty awkward even for those damn birds; soon, they'll fart and crap.

"Changing the subject, squirrel," said Panther, "you might bring a few of your stash of apples for Jamie."

"Yes, that would be nice," said Jamie, as she bumped deliberately into the squirrel who was enjoying some berries himself---strawberries, blueberries, blackberries---that's berry nice. Some of the fruit was fermented more than the others, but there should be choice, and different aging brought a different flavor and sharper taste (quicker drunk) for the select palate.

The pigeons were scattered about the clearing and scatterbrained to begin with, and the others really couldn't tell when they were soused---birds on sauce, bird soup, bombed pigeon, clawed and clumsy---because their shit was the same shit no matter their alcoholic inclinations: white, liquid and plentiful, and very very stinky, no matter what they ate.

Not that Panther's shit didn't stink. But, few would tell him otherwise.

Once the elephant crapped, the smell could reach the Gulf or the Atlantic Ocean and turn the tides back, chase 'em back out. That's smelly. It also wasn't true. The jungle and swamp absorb so many things, including smell.

Talking crap is hilarious. Right? No? Too bad.

"Why don't you say it louder, big guy," said Butts.

"As loud as I feel the need," said Panther.

"I don't need any apples right now," said Jamie, "but later might be nice."

"O.K." said Butts.

"Now!" said Panther.

"Bully!" The squirrel scurried up the branch he was on and leapt to another and was gone and off to the campus, a pre-planned route along and amongst the trees and conifer twigs, branches, and limbs. Just watch the pine needles and sharper-edged leaves, like those of an oak.

Even squirrels cry out in pain, but this one tends to curse, whether hurting or not.

"Ow, shit!" yelled Butts.

"Heard that!" yelled Panther, although the squirrel was already three or four trees away. Now, five.

"Damn kitty!"

"Heard that, too!"

"'Sposeta'!"

"Boys," said Jamie.

Apples, unless the crab kind, are big. Squirrels' mouths are small, their paws not very

Bite it in half, bite it again, and carry the pieces.

A red-tail hawk named Elaine flew circles high in the sky, ready to dive-bomb the crowd, not content to join in the drunken festivities. The raven and crow, Brian and Nathaniel, respectively, stared up into the sky above the clearing from a tree stump near some rotted apples and mangos, but they could've been big cherries and melons. Was she really gonna' dive-bomb again? Never learn. The crow and raven sighed simultaneously.

"She'll come down," said Nathaniel.

"Pass me a bit of mango," said Brian.

"You won't be able to fly."

"I'll hop."

William the pygmy tarsier sat atop Seysew and tugged at an overripe mango and it snapped off a loosened branch that lay next to him. He had to use both hands and feet to manage such an act of bravery, cunning, and alcoholic (and bucolic) behavior. Chimp the chimpanzee and Emily the Angora cat took bites from their plucked and overripe fruits. After such chewing, it was hard to tell from what was left what the fruit had been. It was yellowish, slightly green, perhaps a melon. It didn't matter: They might have hiccups and belching, soon, too.

On the ground, Chipmunk scampered over and grabbed some overripe raspberries.

The pigeons, led by Peter, their alpha, were scattered here and there and overripe with stupidity.

Pantherville: Jamie was the alpha and Panther the beta. Butts was the self-anointed spokesperson; none of the denizens from the 'Ville needed to understand why the tree and nutty rodent was the mouthpiece; no one gave a damn. It could've been Jamieville ... Buttsville ... No: The former sounded like a hospice and the latter a place of ill repute.

Back there, over yonder, through those trees, near the swamp, a hiss loud and clear. Panther looked up and stared in that direction. He'd heard it before on several occasions. He'd investigated but found nothing. Whoever wasn't in the clearing right now wasn't welcome, didn't have his consent. Robert or Roberts or Seysew, she who might stomp on the wrong response (ouch)---none of them might be as patient as the big cat about being an un-invite. Panther needed to know who these dudes were!

Then, more sounds, multiple and omnidirectional from over there, further than that, nearer the swamp, several sources confirmed. Panther barely recognized the sounds, but knew they were from the same animal, several of them, the sounds fractured and dissipating as they echoed through the dense jungle beyond the clearing. He could hear distant twigs and branches snapping, the twigs quick and subtle in their snap, the branches louder with a hollow echo which carried further and past Panther on his limb and beyond.

The hiss, again. Panther had never heard it before, this he knew, had no recollection in his memory bank. He growled low and ominous, a gurgle; deep in his throat. Those in the clearing looked up, aware of the big cat's subtle and chilling alarm. The tall grass, trees, leftover stumps interspersed, from previous lightning strikes, the feet and roots of the jungle, their bodies taken---shoulders, arms, branches, fingers and twigs---creeper vines and figs that choke the life out of the biggest giants like the kapok, much quicker to die by lightning; the bushes that waffle sound up close and down low but also hide shit---literally---the sound of danger heard, for the moment, only by Panther the black jaguar, and the other animals cringed and cowered in response to the alarm, and it was difficult to tell whether the innate fear was initiated with the potential for unwelcome intruders or with the big cat's gurgle and growl---which one is it?---both. *Yes, glad he's on our team.*

Other beasts in the clearing maneuvered, tripping, stumbling, slipping and sliding with fermented fructose rushing through their veins, the metabolism sped up with natural enzymes, what the caveman ate, what the dinosaurs belched with, even the amphibians and fish must've nibbled rotting strawberries, blueberries, raspberries, blackberries floating on the water's surface and settled on fronds just above and lily pads that quilted back and forth and provided homes and resting zones for the drunken and sedentary and swimming beasts.

There's no law in the animal kingdom against swimming while intoxicated. But, you'd think they'd be safer sitting on a lily pad while consuming the fermented fructose.

There's no proof the ancient beasties hiccupped, burped, and had diarrhea from rotting fruit, but nature always finds a way to have Happy Hour. In Pantherville, it was merely a matter of carrying on a tradition of souse.

More animals: The pigeons. There were too many to count. Some sat on the ground, looking like moldy loaves of bread with beaks. The sedentary moldy loaves didn't move except for a twitching butt; and the moldy beakers tripping on their feet, heads bobbing, they twitched their butts, too, as did moldies on branches---they were twitching---and pigeons looking moldy-green tried to fly overhead, but like the much heavier albatrosses (none here), they had a tough time taking off and, in the case of the pigeon, remaining aloft, with little direction; having no excuse except their twitching butts reminded everyone---

"Look out!"

"They're twitching their butts!"

"Watch out!"

"Oh, they're so disgusting!"

---that they were about to take an enormous shit, Elmer's glue-all crap, liquid everywhere, but not yet. *Twitch twitch twitch …*

The other animals began to back off and spread out, ducking, covering their heads with paws, feathers, branches, and snakes don't have feathers or hands … *shit …*

There were no farts with the pigeons---they just pooped, squirting everywhere.

But, not yet.

Fire hoses never had it so good.

"Move out!"

"Go! Go! Go!"

"Outta' here!"

Panther watched and clapped a left paw over his eyes. He hadn't signed up for this. Stinky business: All of them backed off with the impending shit storm. Blame it on the rotting fruit. It was a cheap drunk.

Rachel and Cindy scattered with the rest. Rachel, a panda bear, would've rather have been with Emily the Angora cat, and no one really knew why that was, but in this part of the world, anything was possible---pairings, friendships---exotics: the wildest animals finding kinship with the (formerly) domesticated. Animals get flushed, escape, washed away with hurricanes, tossed out the car on the side of the road, survive somehow through any of these reason/results and become feral, trust humans less, not that they trusted them any more when a pet.

Cindy was a carnivore and one of the best hunters in the kingdom. Pound for pound she might've been stronger than Seysew, or even Panther. Wolverines are fearless and voracious beasts. Jamie could identify; even bears are intimidated by raccoons. Like the panther and wolverine, quickness and sharp claws were keys to the raccoon's survival in the jungle, along with the eyes, olfactory, speed, and luck.

Butts and a scrum of fellow squirrels came dashing, leaping, hopping and crawling along the trees' limbs and branches. They had apples. Chewable cider. Through the trees, along the branches, scaling limbs on the spruce because pine needles made for difficult trespass and many squirrels didn't care much for pine cones. Some squirrels ate the pine nuts within, but not Butts and the other grays.

Ten squirrels pulled up to a stop in an oak tree, occupied several branches, apple chunks in their cheeks, all of it for Jamie the raccoon. With the aging of the apples in mind, she must really appreciate a good apple cider.

Happy Hour in *this* jungle included delivery.

The squirrels looked down at the clearing, now dispersed or evacuated on account of the pigeons, who were still there, leaving this paragraph in peril, turmoil, oxymoronic---cleared out, but not really. But! They hadn't dumped, yet.

Panther didn't give a crap that the pigeons were about to dump. He was far enough away. But, the other animals were closer, if only by yards. When the pigeons dumped, there was a lot more to worry about than the clearing. The impending shit storm would affect a much wider expanse. It would be mayhem, a very sloppy and smelly one.

Panther really wasn't far enough away.

"We're running!" yelled several animals. Where? The pigeons do know how to fly ... and shit. How far could they fly and shit? They weren't that big. But, they had a lot of shit.

Chipmunk had joined Emily, Chimp, and Cindy on top of Seysew. She raised her trunk and turned her tusks in the opposite direction, letting out a trumpeting blast in protest, her trunk straight out and pointed *that* way, where she wished to head, away from so many dirty birds, who hadn't shit quite yet.

Robert and Roberts, however brave and fearsome like Seysew and Panther, slid and crawled, respectively, alongside the African elephant, equally at a loss as to how far they needed to be in order not to be skunked and soaked by the pigeon super-stink.

There is no skunk drunk and big enough to match so many flying dirty moldy loaves with beaks and their inebriated and diarrhetic state-of-mind.

Jamie and Butts, Brian and Nathaniel, Rachel; Seysew with William, Chimp, and Emily up top---all were already closer to the swamp, where the odors of life and death and poo-poo from other beasties in and out of the murky water were a lot easier to bear. No shit smells worse than the pigeons'. (Just ask the other animals.) Indeed, skunk cabbage, bog rot and rotting fish had nothing on pigeon odor. Run *far* away when they're ready to dump!

Elaine was joined far overhead by the crow and raven. William had leapt from the elephant and climbed high in a kapok.

"Way up there?!" yelled Chimp.

"They *stink*!!" yelled William.

"If they fly over??"

"Whatever!!

When the pigeons decided to take flight (a few already had tried but were unsuccessful, inebriated), no one was safe. All the pigeons were earthbound, some on the lower limbs (O.K., a few had managed to crash-land *above*-ground) and branches of conifers, oak, ash, apple and elm, and that one giant kapok. The rest of the shit-beaks lolled, sprawled, and drunkenly lollygagged on the clearing's craggy turf, debilitated with putrid alcoholic and rotting fruit. Everyone knew what the pigeons were going to fart and shit; *this* was a foregone conclusion … inescapable.

Peter the alpha pigeon was approached; the first and second lieutenants now stood in front of him. The smell of methane was in the air. The farting was underway. The situation was dire, at least for everyone else, except maybe the earthworms.

Other than the pigeons and earthworms, it was bedlam: A drunken, mad rush to get out further out of the way, and while the pigeons met to discuss their smell, many of the animals wondered, *Am I far enough*? … *maybe not* … and they spread out, fanning out, while reminding themselves and each other that they were still enjoying Happy Hour (see the way they're stumbling, much like the pigeon horde) however interrupted by hundreds (so many) of stinking-up-the-joint pigeons.

"I'm over here!" yelled Roberts.

"That's not far enough!" yelled Robert.

"What's beyond the swamp?!" cried Seysew.

"Hey, I'm tiny!" cried William. "What about asphyxiation?"

"Don't be ridiculous!" yelled Rachel. "They *couldn't* be that odiferous!"

"Yes!!" yelled the others. "They can!!"

"They will!!" reiterated the trumpeting Seysew (she's a huge elephant, but can get shat upon), sounding off as she trampled on by, piggy-backing Chimp, Emily, Chipmunk and William, who'd decided further away didn't mean climbing higher, because the heat from a pigeon shit-flood rises, the stink necessarily along with it.

Yeah, the pigeons can fly over trees, too.

Panther stared out over the jungle with both eyes open. He wasn't concerned with the stink-bombing of the clearing and the jungles surrounding it, and the stink would reach him. He'd smelt so much worse---death and rotting corpses. The wrath-like mayhem of a hurricane and its withdrawal and the destruction and death it leaves behind, the smell of residue. He'd seen *residue*. Getting shat upon wasn't very glorious, *uh uh*. But ... *It will rain soon enough*. No. He wasn't concerned about the busting up of Happy Hour; they'd return tomorrow, another Rotting-Fruit Festival.

He heard the hissing again, multiple, layered; it sounded like a waterfall with many rock ledges and huge hollowed-out lagoon beneath, the water falling in there; the sound of so many rock crevasses as the water fell, bounced and slapped here and there, cacophony, and the hissing in its dangerous symphony sounded just like that---at least, to Panther it did. He knew the jungle, and he knew this hissing sound didn't belong around here. Then again, he wasn't from here, either. All Jungles did not sound the same. Panther knew this, instinctively.

He growled, a low sound, about as low as a hollowed-out lagoon. The pigeons froze, hundreds or thousands of them. The other animals heard it, too, the growl, and they stopped where they were at. A black jaguar's gurgle carries pretty damn far, very low on the sound registry, like echoing thunder into the distance.

No one but Panther heard the hissing, like it was meant for his ears only. If anyone else heard it, they might not discern the danger. The big cat knew.

"Commander?" *Hiccup*

"Yes, first lieutenant," said Peter pigeon. *Fart*

"I think we've reached a point of inebriation from which there is no return."

"What's that mean, lieutenant?"

"We're soused, sir."

"What does the second lieutenant have to say about this?"

"He's pretty soused, too ... *Hiccup* ... sir."

"I'm right here, commander." The second lieutenant lifted himself off a pile or scrum of six or seven drunken stinkin' rotten fellow pigeons. He stumbled the five feet of approach to the first lieutenant and commander. That's 50 to 60 feet relative to a human, stumbling along after getting off a human pile of drunken sots, reporting for duty, or not. Happy Hour is a tough business for bird and man ... elephants ... squirrels ... alligators ... chimpanzees.

You can barely walk," said Peter.

"Or, talk---*hiccup*---sir."

"Sir," said the first lieutenant, "we can't---*fart*---last much longer."

"Must we have this problem every time?" said Peter.

"We're pigeons, sir---*belch*---it's what we do, or cannot do ... *Hiccup* ... Something like that."

Panther was tuned to a rhythmic if not continuous hiss, interrupted by a bark like a dog or something, a yelp like a hyena, or an old-fashioned iron radiator sending out steam, very hot, with occasional clanking as the metal within expands and contracts.

Then again, a jaguar wouldn't know anything about radiators having never lived in the North. Then again, Panther is like a radiator: He gets hot and blows off steam, too.

Panther didn't know metal from bamboo and didn't need to. He was all about the jungle and being alert and ready. The jungle had its own heat and steam from the humidity and danger and constant threat; the radiator may be made of iron, perhaps indestructible, but the jungle was a lot more dangerous, and the jaguar wasn't indestructible. He crawled along the limb and readied himself to leap. He'd had some of the Happy Hour fruit, but affects from his share of the rotting-fruit wealth had dissipated. He was ready. Bring on the hiss.

The other animals, unaware of any hissing, radiator- or jungle-style and blithe in their fruity spirits, did remain aware enough of an impending and imminent methane attack.

"Why can't we behave like normal birds and just fly away?!"

"Commander," said the first lieutenant, "sometimes you just gotta' go ... sir." He flew up to join the others, thousands of them, they who'd suddenly had the impetus to take off and shit. The time to shit coincided with their ability to get up there and let it all fall from above. Yep, there they went. Ready?

"Commander," said the second lieutenant. "I can't hold it any longer."

"O.K., O.K.," said Peter. "Let's go. I really don't have to *go*---you know, *that* kind of 'go'---"

"Not enough fruit and fiber, sir!" yelled the first lieutenant as he circled rather haphazardly overhead, jerking back and forth, struggling, his flight pattern more erratic by the second. Flying and crapping at the same time: Can't be easy.

It was time.

"How do they *do* that?" said Jamie, strain in her voice. She tried not to sniff.

"What---shit?" said Chipmunk.

"We've got problems if they come this way," said Butts.

Hundreds of pigeons arced higher and higher---no, they were stumbling in mid-air, jousting and jostling---and they struggled to reach their zeniths in flight, ramming into each other, and they began to lose their grip with flight, slipping, falling, … screw 'em …

… "Wow, that is really disgusting" … "Grotesque" … "The trees will never be the same" … "Uh uh, just needs to rain, but in the meantime, pretty gross, yeah" … The stink was proliferative and … "pretty gross."

Thousands of pigeons (wait … How many?) let loose their propaganda of poop, shit spread everywhere; even the animals that had scattered on the ground and by air, escaped to their respective peripheries---where they thought they were safe from the pigeon plop---were mindful that the pigeons can't seem to aim, whether by flight or by dumping (forget both at the same time), they and their caca land where they do (blame it on Happy Hour), droppings anywhere and everywhere, a nuclear methane bombastic (whatever that means)---the denizens of Pantherville weren't far enough away from the peril of a huge caca drop. The stink might permeate the jungle. Nothing lasts long here, not in this heat and humidity, but these are pigeons. They didn't just drop it all, they coated everything, like a huge swath of icing on lemon cake. Nothing would be the same for a while---well, at least 10 minutes or so.

The pigeons, so many, were scattered above the jungle floor as they found themselves lighter and flying higher with their release; they flew away, the further the better, as the rest of the animals and Panther, still on his limb on the other side, sighed, a collective sigh of relief. Caution: The stink might back up with a breeze. There was no breeze. This time, nobody got coated. The smell stayed away, dissipating further into the jungle on the other side of the clearing from Panther's limb.

"I got a lot of apples," said Butts, as he surveyed the "White Out", gallons of wet farts---yeah, dumps---covering most of the clearing and dripping off the trees surrounding the no-longer-edible and rotting fruit. Saving graces: There'd be more fruit to fall, and Panther's tree had been far enough away the other way to avoid the drip-flop … -shit.

"I think we need a thunderstorm," said Cindy.

"Soon," said Jamie. "Hopefully, soon."

"Fine," said Chipmunk. "I'll hail the clouds and humidity, and you bring the breeze, squirrel."

Humidity: Here. Breeze: Not.

Panther grunted.

"I see thick clouds over there," cried Elaine as her voice carried over the survivors, her Doppler Effect's voice sounding as she swooped right to left.

"Wow," said Nathaniel as he flew the other way, the Doppler now in stereo, "we might get rain."

"Imagine that," said Brian, as he dropped some blackberries, quite unintentionally, and cursed to himself for not getting drunker at the earliest opportunity and having to retrieve on the ground, which was slathered in white slop.

"Was that necessary?" said Jamie. She did not appreciate cursing.

"I'll pick them up and eat 'em."

"Never mind."

Panther stared at the mess. He no longer heard the distant hiss. Perhaps, the creatures couldn't run that fast or fly; pigeon shit and its stink can be suffocating. Perhaps, they'd had their share of rotting fruit somewhere else and had passed out, if not passed on. Dead strangers, uninvited, he had no problem with, not now, not any day.

Bring on the weather and clean up the latest mess.

He sighed and laid back down on one of a kapok tree's huge limbs, the lowest of the tree, about 20 feet up and 40 feet long including its branches and leafy twigs.

As the pigeons scattered to distant points unimagined and no one cared about (nor did they care about the caca-drippers), and the other animals kind of wondered how methane could cause such a reaction (not much to wonder about: light a match and *boom*), Peter and his two lieutenants managed to assess their situation on-the-wing and flapping flopping and sometimes flipping in mid-air though not flipping off each other.

Peter: "I think we should reassess our comportment vis a vis our visitations at Happy Hour."

First Looey: "What'd he say?" *Flap Flop ... flip.*

Second Looey: "I don't know." *Flop flip ... flap.*

Peter: "We shouldn't partake of the rotting fruit in light of the resultant and diarrhea fiasco."

First Looey: "What'd he *say*??"

Second Looey: "I still don't know."

The mass of pigeons, hundreds if not thousands of them (really, no one needs to count---no one), found themselves drifting over the Florida Bay, having disposed of enough shit to fill an airplane hangar, maybe one big enough to house a 747 ... O.K., maybe just a really really small corner of the same hangar, but that's still a *lot*, dammit'.

Panther sniffed the air once or twice, his eyes turning orange from what wafted on the warm breeze---sooner or later, the crap-breeze had to come this way. He closed his eyes. He couldn't close his nostrils, but they'd smelt worse---like the rotting of corpses in the debris left over from a hurricane.

"You think the next time we don't invite those guys?" said Butts.

"They weren't invited this time," said Seysew, "so it doesn't matter."

"There are no invites, squirrel," said the big cat, "but we are careful about strangers."

"They mean no harm," said Jamie. "The pigeons, that is."

"Yeah, they're so stupid, that's all," said Chipmunk.

"That's not nice."

"What else would you call it?" said Chimp.

"Everyone goes to the bathroom, smart or stupid," said Emily.

"Not like that. They crap like a huge crack in the dam; there's no end to it."

"That's because there're so many," said Cindy.

"Too many, indeed," said Rachel.

"They crap like they're twice as many," said William, the tiniest of observers.

"So they have to show up at once?!" said Butts. "What happened to eating in shifts?"

"You mean," said Chipmunk, "getting drunk in shifts."

"You're going to tell them this, squirrel?" said Jamie.

"I've never gotten drunk in a *shift*---I just get drunk when I get drunk," said Rachel.

"No, I'm going to eat an apple," said Butts, and then he sniffed the air as he stared wide-eyed at everyone in turn. "Don't light a match---*anyone*."

Jamie managed to stifle a laugh, a snort, whatever, but the others could not. She might've giggled.

Panther, with his keen hearing, along with keen smell and sight, shook his head. He kept his eyes closed. A storm was brewing. The methane had no chance once the dump was dissipated and dissolved into the earth. Jungles are green and thick and wet for several reasons, one of which was overwhelming right now, the other which was due soon for clean-up duty.   Shit and rain: They go together and help things grow ... together.

    Damn pigeons.

    Hurry up, thunderstorm.

Chapter 2: Irritating Species As Clams, Pigeons & Ants

She took a bite of the apple and chewed. Of course, it wasn't the whole thing, it was a chunk. The squirrels' jaws are only so big. But, it was a sizeable chunk, about a fifth, large enough to get immersed in the meat and its fermenting juices, and Jamie had no problem with fermenting juices. She was a lush like all the rest of the beasties. Good job carrying those chunks of apples, squirrels.

The thunderstorm had come and gone and done its job. The only way to tell that the pigeons had again shown they can't handle their liquor was their current condition. Hundreds huddled along the clearing, sapped of their strength, hungover, belching and hiccupping, trying to fart out of reflex but no sound and, most important, no stink (give it up, birds), their colons flushed, Too-Much-Information in the jungle ... moaning and groaning pigeons, so much to learn about the consumption of fermenting berries, apples, mangos, but no bananas around here. No one knew how to make daiquiris, anyway.

The Florida Everglades, its jungles and swamps (and further south, the Keys) were guaranteed two thunderstorms a day from May through September, as regular as pigeon shit.

The pigeons could crap all they want, but it was their problem if they couldn't learn from their mistakes: Some animals can't handle their alcohol. The clearing never looked worse than when the horde of flying garbage bins decided to overdo it (too much fruit … again), then find themselves debilitated (plastered) and out-of-sorts (hungover and diarrhetic) afterward. No one knew whether they were that stupid that they couldn't figure out on a daily basis that their stomachs were only so big and bad blood sugar and alcoholic poisoning can make anyone really sick---and look really *stupid*.

Jamie crawled along a beaten path through the jungle. Keeping her company were Panther, Butts, and Chipmunk---he, for lack of foot speed, rode on the big cat's back. Butts scattershot and scooted over the limbs and branches and even the twigs of the trees, the twigs twinging and snapping back upon his leaping and hopping departure; with his agility and adept ability and balance could move rather quickly and already been on the beach, but slowed his navigational speed in order to allow the others to pace. He knew if he sped ahead Jamie would get angry. Panther didn't care. He could outpace them all.

Them: Jamie and Butts.

"How can I have a conversation with you if you take off like that?"

"I don't know. Wait until you get there and tell me then."

Wrong answer, squirrel.

Panther was alert for the *sound*, the hissing he'd heard earlier. Perhaps, the storm had satisfied their curiosity, that Pantherville was safe from intrusion by unwanted outsiders; those that didn't understand (sure, they did) or didn't want to abide by the watering-hole ethic which, according to the jaguar, applied to Pantherville, even though there wasn't a natural watering present ... Herein: *No one's allowed to eat anyone else at the watering holes, clearing, or, in his, Panther's, territory, which encompassed the jungle to its perimeters abutting the encroaching suburb, college campus, power plant and its canals, and the swamp.* Well put, jaguar. No, there weren't any watering holes nearby, but still well-said.

He heard another sound, this one somewhat familiar and feral, and perhaps bigger than he. Panther had grown up in captivity in Brazil, where he was born in the wild before being captured. He knew a lot about all kinds of big cats like himself, some smaller like cheetahs and larger like a male lion or Bengal tiger. He would keep these new and feral sounds to himself. As long as the others didn't react, he figured they figured it was just the jungle and its sounds, not always friendly, but sometimes the sounds come from bigger and more dangerous and desperate animals than Panther. They figured he'd take care of these "more dangerous and desperate animals than Panther."

Watering hole, clearing and his territory in general had to be always ready for intruders, invaders with dangerous intent. All had to be on alert. It was, after all, a jungle out there.

Yeah, no watering hole. But, sometimes the flooding makes it seem that way.

"You look distracted," said Jamie as she waddled along.

"Too many berries, I guess," said Panther.

"I ate more than you," said Chipmunk, "and I'm fine." *Hiccup*

"Just ride up there and shut up."

"Aren't we grumpy," said Jamie.

"Nah---Am I?"

"Well, the usual riffraff showed up at Happy Hour, and everyone nearly got shat upon---again."

"Those pigeons aren't full of shit anymore."

Jamie giggled.

"There's always tomorrow."

"Thank goodness for daily rain."

Butts scampered through the trees' upward reaches, at times tiptoeing along the conifers' branches because pine needles smart, can hurt, but for the most part scampering, leaping, landing on the end of a twig and boomeranging deeper into the heart of an oak, maple or elm, springing out the other side, a trapeze artist very small, a squirrel with a bushy tail, one who hoards apples and claims a clearing for himself, but---

"Hey, big cat!" Butts was stopped at the end of a branch that jutted out over a sand dune that overflowed into the woods. Just how good is sand for the trees when it overflows into the woods? Only the sand and trees know for sure. The other side of the dune sloped down to the water's edge 20 feet away.

Panther stopped at the end of the trail just before the sand, which was in layers on top of the jungle floor---sand, gravel, rocks, all the same; sand and dirt (same), even the detritus which turned to a fiber-laden mess when it rained (mud); even the shit, even the dead animals; fecal matter and dead matter all mattered the same, however the semantics.

Panther grew up in Brazil, where he was a captive audience with many other exotic animals (mostly other and various big cats) to a contractor magnate. Eventually, he was sold to a zoo up north in Florida. One day, the truck carrying him crashed while on the way to the zoo. Butts happened to be nearby and came scurrying up to the crash site. He approached the injured black jaguar, all eight feet and 250 pounds of him, and urged him on, to get away, escape, and be free. The squirrel had a lot of guts, but he saw a fellow animal, however huge, in distress. Panther could've eaten him for a snack, but realized that the squirrel was trying to help him live. He really hadn't wanted to eat the rodent, anyway: junk food.

Now, here he was at the edge of the jungle, crossing the sand, with Chipmunk riding his back and Butts awaiting his response. Jamie kept on toward the water, mindful of what could lurk in there.

"I'm here," said Panther.

"I suppose we're gathering some food."

"Wanna' go fishing?"

"Not if they're still there," and the squirrel pointed down the beach and out over the breaking waves, however small they were, about three feet high. Further out, a roiling mass of water, busy with activity, so many fish, not very friendly, sharp teeth---piranha.

"Ahhhh, yes," said Panther. "Well, they're in their element, aren't they?"

Chipmunk hopped off Panther---

"Ouch."

"Sorry."

Claws …

---and headed in the direction of the piranha-mosh, all four inches of him, not with the intention of joining in, but perhaps inclined to taunt. After all, as long as he didn't decide to go swimming, he didn't have to worry about them coming closer to shore and responding to his taunting. Most fish out of water don't prefer to be there, including the piranha. Chipmunk: Don't go in the water.

"Leave them alone, Chipmunk," said Jamie.

"I just wanna' say 'Hello'."

"Don't think you'll get a reply."

"Get away from them, dude!" said Butts. "Don't irritate them!"

"How can you tell the difference?" said Panther as he lay on the nearest sand dune and began to nod off.

"They don't have feet, Butts!" said Chipmunk.

Jamie usually had a brood with her, or Panther and Butts babysat in her absence. Sometimes, she'd needed her rest. But, it appeared that after years of birthing and raising her annuals, she was done. Only she knew for sure. Some thought the only reason why the squirrel and her were friends was he provided apples. He was good for: babysitting and apples. Otherwise, there was no reason for them to be friends. Raccoons: very private. Squirrels: Irritating as shit, but not quite as bad as clams, ants, and pigeons.

It was thought they got along because she'd set up house and home the last few years in his territory (She'd needed his permission??) underneath a porch attached to a suburban home. He never thought of telling her to find a home elsewhere (He could tell her that?!) because she'd kick his butt in a fight. (That's more like it ...)

Panther's whiskers twitched. He felt something underneath his hairy belly. He sniffed the air and pricked his ears. He lifted his torso from the sand dune and stared at the sight underneath.

"Excuse me," he said. "I'll move."

A clam attempted to crawl or slither---manuever---across the sand. He seemed out of breath.

"Buddy, why don't you watch where you're lounging!"

"I'm sorry." Panther kept his torso raised as other clams emerged from the damp dune (remember the thunderstorm) and began their snail's pacing.

Several more spoke up at once or nearly so, a rapid-fire conversation, and it's really tough to hear them breathing, even for Panther's sensitive ears.

"I couldn't breathe!"

"You big *lummox*!"

"Lose some weight, buster!"

"Why don't ya' look where you're sitting next time!"

Panther laid back down with a vengeance, the full force of his 250 pounds.

Crunch ... It got quiet.

Panther lifted his body again. "Sorry."

"Dinner!" yelled Jamie as she surveyed the dampened dune and its shell-full remains.

"Yeah, I didn't mean to but I did."

"Oh well, I would've done so on purpose."

"Maybe, I did." Panther gave his Cheshire-like grin.

Butts came scurrying up. The piranha pod had moved further down the beach.

Panther would get Roberts to maul them a little later, providing another good dinner for the alligator. He'd eaten them before; it'd been quite a scene.

"I'm supposed to like clams, right?" said the squirrel as he came to a stop and sat, his whiskers twitching. About the only thing he had in common with the big cat: twitching whiskers.

Without the usual raccoon brood to babysit, Panther and Butts didn't know what to do with themselves besides organizing Happy Hour, sleeping, eating, and picking on each other. It was nearly mid-summer in the jungle, and the Dog Days applied to anybody and anything that had a heartbeat or grew out of the ground, trees, and cracks in the sidewalks. You can only hope that they've learned their lesson from this Happy Hour: some animals in the kingdom cannot handle their rotting-fruit consumption and don't know when to stop; when enough is enough.

"I thought you didn't eat seafood?" asked Butts.

"I don't," replied Panther. "It was an accident!"

"You accidentally killed lunch?"

"You know, if Jamie decides not to have any more kids, she might base the decision on the way you turned out, squirrel."

"At least I don't hurt clams---I mean, that's wimpy."

"I love them," said Jamie, as she slurped up the clam meat.

"I wasn't *hunting*---I fell!" said Panther.

"Yeah, it's easy to fall on the beach," said Butts. "Sand: slippery."

Panther raised an eyebrow and sighed. Jamie continued to slurp.

The squirrel scanned the beach, looking for a tree, any tree, however dead.

"I don't see a limb, big guy, dead or alive."

"The sand is 'slippery,' like you said!"

"I was dripping sarcasm---drip drip drip."

"Drip *this*, rodent!"

"Boys." *Slurp*.

"I don't normally eat squirrel."

"I'm 'junk food'---Remember?"

"Boys."

Overhead, there were so many pigeons flying out of formation---well, they don't know *formation*, but they do know how to shit anywhere and make a huge mess wherever they go, the Florida summer thunderstorms their saving grace this time---again---*Where're we going? How do we fly? What happened?* Some dudes should not drink.

They were discombobulated by rotting fruit and lightning bolts, the static in the air. Now, if they'd actually get hit ... (That's not nice.)

Perhaps they shouldn't be invited to any more Pantherville Happy Hours. Several landed near the water's edge, including Peter and his two lieutenants. They eyed the clam meat on the dune.

"Don't even *think* about it," said Panther.

The rest of the pigeons flew out over the ocean and pretended to mingle with the terns and gulls and actually scared the crap out of the piranha (they didn't actually shit) who scattered then reformed because instinct told them to. The pigeons had no clue where they were, if they ever do, besotted or not, but there were so many of the winged shit-stormers that they looked like a cumulo-pigeon or fog-bank-pigeon or flying wet-and-mildewed leaves ... flying *yucks*.

"Sir, I think the rest have no clues what to do," said the first lieutenant who, himself, has never had one. (That's not nice.)

"What do you want from me?" said Peter as he bobbed in a circle not far from the two-to three-foot breakers. To a pigeon, that's a tidal wave; to an ant, a tsunami ... Panther took care of the clams. Next ...

"O.K., boys," said the ant commander. "We've a job to do, so let's do it!"

"Let's *doo iiiiiiiitt!!*" cried the ant masses, having no idea what "It" might have been; having no idea they mimicked a character in a famous movie. Heading for the waves, boys?

"What?!" cried Panther as he stared at the several-inches-wide insect stream that moved pretty damn quick for inch-long creatures with pretty short legs; if the big cat could run that fast relative to his size, he'd be scooting at 100 miles per hour. He could pass the cheetah.

"Grab all you can, boys; it's fresh-kill, you know!"

Panther watched as the quick-moving multitude grabbed the clam meat and disappeared with their fresh stash into the tall grass two feet away. From the time they arrived until returning to the grass---15 seconds.

"I saw what I saw," Panther said.

"What *was* that?!" said Jamie as she had stepped back, hopped, to avoid the tiny creepy crawlers.

"Ants," said Butts, as he chomped a chunk of apple that had been in a cheek pouch. "They're all over the campus." He shivered.

The pigeons flew away from the sea birds, who'd been cursing throughout the interruption, with little exchange of words, very little communication, an invasion of the sea birds' territory, and again Peter and his lieutenants landed near the waters' edge. It was still so very warm and they needed to get their padded feet wet. Terns and seagulls and other beach-bird stalwarts continued their cursory screeching, and the piranha weren't about to turn around and investigate---yeah, even they know to stay away from junk food.

"Ya' think Roberts might wanna' confront the piranha?" said Butts.

"Not usually," said Panther. "That one time was an emergency. If it's not easy to catch, he's not really interested."

"They're just fish."

"Fine, you catch them."

"I don't eat fish."

"Catch 'em, anyway---for Roberts."

"I don't like fish."

"Wimp."

"C'mon, big guy, they're almost as big as me."

"Find more clams."

"I'm fine, Panther," said Jamie. "The apples are enough. You guys can stop fighting

for a while."

"We're not fighting."

"Nope," said Butts. "You drunk, yet?"

"Drunk enough to think you're handsome," laughed Panther.

"That was mean," said Jamie.

"Sorry."

"No, you're not," said the squirrel.

"No, I'm not, you're right; I'm not apologizing to you."

"We can't all be big and brutish like you, big guy."

Millions of ants came streaming out of the tall grass (again), spread out 10 feet long and about three feet wide, 30 feet square, so many irritating little creatures. They belched as one and it sounded like a grunting gorilla, which isn't that loud, but certainly pretty scary, about as scary (when it's actually a gorilla grunting)---scarier maybe than the gurgle of a black jaguar while lying on a kapok fig tree limb. Then, they farted as one, millions of them, sounding like a truck horn, a big truck, an 18-wheeler carrying an oversized power unit or part of a jet engine or something really big-ass, but a millions-strong ant-fart, however brief, but effective, smelly, gross. Then they departed as quickly as they'd arrived (again), kind of like a fast-moving subway train, including the Doppler affect, at rush hour in New York City, downtown, right to left, and the ants, so many, moved like that, taking their huge belch and stinky fart with them---well not really, belches are wet and farts are residual, sometimes wet, too---apparently, pigeon farts and shit have nothing on the intensity, however brief, regarding millions of nearly inch-long army ants burping and farting as one.

"We could never be that organized, or that smelly," said Butts. "We don't have the wherewithal."

"'Wherewithal'?!" exclaimed Panther. "Like, we'd *plan* that??"

"I would've warned them about eating clams too fast, but they wouldn't have listened---*men*!" said Jamie.

"They're *ants*!"

"They're as irritating as the pigeons."

"No, they're not." The big cat nodded toward the mass of pigeons, which tended to blot out the sun in their movement, this kind of movement, flight, more acceptable than their bowel movements, flying haphazard, looping, dropping, lifting; they'd even frightened the piranha who had to re-form their spinning ball of death, however an imbroglio.

Stink will always conquer spinning balls of death.

"I didn't think such tiny critters could raise such a stink," said Jamie.

"The pigeons' or the ants'?" said Butts.

"You've never smelt your pups' poop?" said Panther.

"That's not nice," said Jamie.

"Why are we still here?" said Butts.

"It's just methane," said Panther. "It won't kill you. Carbon monoxide---that kills."

"What happened to the imbroglio?"

"The ... *What*?"

"The piranha ..." Butts glanced around, then down at the sand, toed it. "I know words."

"What *about* them?"

"They're disorganized but deadly. I'm surprised they don't eat themselves."

"I wish the pigeons would eat themselves," said Jamie.

"That's 'not nice,' either."

"That's mean," said Panther.

"No," said Jamie. "It's not." She sniffed.

"They can't," said the squirrel. "They're herbivorous."

"They're *what*?!---Where do you get these words??" huffed Panther.

"Campus."

"Well, keep it *there*!"

"Boys."

The pigeons began to land in a haphazard way (What else do they know??): falling, not diving, plopping; not very sure-footed.

Peter and his lieutenants stared into the tall grass, where the ants had gone.

"We're not getting any more clams if we don't move fast enough," said Peter.

"I thought we don't eat meat," said the first lieutenant.

"Clams aren't meat, they're seafood," said the second lieutenant.

"Shellfish."

"Whatever."

"Yeah, but we still have to chew. We don't have teeth."

A sound, like that of a Texas shower, its drops huge and plentiful, very cold and falling fast, and this sound wouldn't stop, not for many minutes, and the earth shook not from the individual drops but from the multitude of drops almost as one, and some, many did land simultaneously, and with the landing of so many thousands there came a secondary sound, a release of air, methane, cubic feet of gas, which was aimed toward the waves, scattering fish, and the animals on the beach were fortunate because, although shaken by the landing, the emissions of the thousands of drunken pigeons went the other way. No one died in the water, either, but asphyxiation was a possibility.

"Hey, boss, I think we got a problem."

"What's that," said the commandant of the ants.

The first lieutenant stared at the second lieutenant, which amounted to full recognizance once their antennae had established contact with each other, which occurs in milliseconds, but for the sake of staring, perhaps those milliseconds were delayed for milliseconds. There are no numbers available for how many times a minute (let alone per day … wow, many many many) ants communicated via antennae contact, whether with each other while identifying any danger or food or friend in their proximity.

"Pigeons," the two lieutenants replied in unison.

The commandant peered out of the tall grass toward the dune and, although many ant species do not see well, these were carpenter ants (army ants, carpenter ants, they're all irritating, like the pigeons, clams and, oh yeah, piranha … and Butts) and were capable of seeing in the daytime to a certain degree. (So, they're carpenter ants … fine.) Their night vision: much better.

"I can't see over the top of the dune, but I saw them---smelled them---flying."

"So many," said the first lieutenant.

"We are more," said the second lieutenant.

Their collective antennae: Busy.

"Why are they here?" asked Jamie.

"Food," said Panther. "They'll eat anything---Squirrel? You find more clams?"

"Over here, I found more bubbling holes."

The pigeons, so many, turned and stared as one at the squirrel's pronouncement.

The ants, so many more, scampered across the sand and stopped not far from the squirrel, who didn't give a damn about the pigeons, ants, piranha, or the clams; even though he had a pretty good idea himself what it was like to be an irritating animal.

"Oh, dear," said Jamie, "so many beasties here."

"Indeed," said Panther.

"I'm *not* digging them up!" yelled Butts.

"I got this."

"*What* do you 'got'?"

The squirrel stared dumbstruck as the big cat landed hard on the wet sand nearer the surf, and so many clams popped to the surface, at least curious (too badda' for them), and Panther landed again, a belly flop---**CRUNCH!!**

The pigeons all at once said "Oooooh!"

Jamie said, "That's my big kitty."

"Show off!" yelled Butts.

The ants shifted gears and headed toward the fresh "meat" and so many piranhas reformed near the shore. (Who's gonna' toss them food?) Panther roared and they scattered, punching through the breaking waves as they did. Pigeons flew, a scattershot, the sky dark overhead as their masses blocked out the late afternoon sun. They eyed the crunched clams and there wasn't nearly enough for them. Panther roared skyward and suddenly there was a late-afternoon sun again. The ants were a huge blot on the sand, their antennae very busy. They'd stopped with the first roar and nearly peed their pants---if they'd been wearing any. Of course, they weren't, so they could've peed into the sand; it was very possible. With the second roar, there was no doubt they'd peed: The damp sand smelt of ant piss.

"That stinks as much as the pigeons do," said Butts with a sniff.

Panther turned to the millions of tiny animals that had spread out.

"Boo!"

"That doesn't scare us, you big meany!" said the first lieutenant.

The big cat stomped on the sand one more time. (Or flopped … whatever.)

Ants. Dispersed. Gone.

Jamie looked at the feast of clams. "I'm hungry," she said.

The squirrel smelled his own urine in the wet sand.

Panther sniffed and grinned.

"It's all the fruit I ate," said Butts.

"Whatever," said Panther.

Chapter 3: Amsterdam Meets Naja & Vice-Versa

The moon seemed to hover over Pantherville, like it was stalking and alive---as bright as a full moon could be, and the trouble and drama and weirdness a full moon can bring to the jungle, where there is enough trouble without the help of a hovering full moon. Panther remained on alert as dusk settled, a leftover mauve from the sunset over there, west. The big cat watched with bright yellow eyes as the moon slowly slid along its arc in the sky.

The summer's daytime humidity gave no quarter to the night air and remained behind to blanket the earth and sky with moisture. The moon floated above the jungle humidity, or maybe it was underwater, as it vibrated and throbbed through the veil of dense air, but there's no swimming in the sky. The animals looked up, looked through the nearly opaque humidity, their eyes glowing with the effervescence, witnessed the perception of floating, or it was swimming up there, the mind's-eye couldn't be sure, or maybe it was just enjoying the imagining, the imagery.

For many of the jungle beasts, it was a time for hunting or getting eaten, and close calls. They didn't give a crap about any floating going on in the sky, only that it was bright and brought out the craziness in all living things.

That was a *Thump*! It wasn't as loud as the thumps Panther had heard earlier, and it didn't reverberate like earlier. This thump wasn't grounded. It was higher, like it came from the trees. Nearby, it was. It could be the moon was dancing, bumping into the trees.

Thump! *Thump*! *Thump*!

Then a *hissssssss* …

What? Panther leapt to the ground, a hardscrabble surface, uneven terrain, plenty of roots going every which way, but the big cat landed like a domestic, all 250 pounds of him, soft landing, ready. He smelt mischief and sulfur, an incoming thunderhead about to give the jungle and swamp, power plant, suburbs, bay and college campus beyond its nightly summer burst of weather. He knew he was better off up in the tree, a large-limbed oak that had been around since the 19th century. Panther knew nothing about centuries or what an oak was, but he did know all about defending and surviving.

Thump! *Splash*! *Ker-thunk*!

Hissssssss ...

What??

Booming thunder, closer now, over the swamp where lightning hit a submerged boulder---

Craaaaaakkkkkk---kkk---k---kkkk ...

---*Ouch! That* hurt, as the terrain beneath him jumped like it was in pain as well---*Buhbuhbuhbuhbuhbooom ... boomboomboomboom*---thunder shook the earth and trees and animals and waterways and sounded like so many stones in a wooden box seesawing back and forth, and Godzilla held the huge container with his paws and claws and shook it, shake shake shake.

Panther might've asked, "Who is Godzilla?"

"Who goes there?" Panther did ask. He didn't recognize the voice, very low, so low, a deep register, down there, resounding, guttural, big guy, big big ... **big** ... and the pelting rains began, big swollen drops, cold. He should climb back up to the limb. This ... this new "voice" wasn't important in this weather. He'd figure it out later.

Snap! Too quick to see what he felt and heard, but nothing actually touched or struck him. No sting. Nothing.

What? The terrain got slippery in a hurry as large goose-shit-sized raindrops fell to the earth through the trees' leaves, bouncing off the limbs, branches, bending twigs perpendicular, right-angled to the ground for only a moment, the trees dancing with the impact, the suddenness and rapidity of the huge raindrops, landing hard and cold, fast and rapid on Panther as he---

Snap! Lunge! Grab! Snap! Squirm!

The huge snake's *hissssssss* could barely be heard through the roar of the Texas shower and, however muted, it was ominous, threatening, confident and warning of a deadliness not seen in these parts since, well, the big black jaguar called Panther came along.

"I got him---her---not sure which!" said the huge beast. A gigantic snake whirled, twisted, and squirmed in his big right paw's grasp.

"You're a ... gorilla," said Panther.

"That's right," he said. "Stop it or I'll rip you in half!" He was speaking to the snake who continued his or her irate and irritating behavior.

"Thank you," said the big cat.

"For what?"

"For keeping me from killing that serpent."

"Doubt that; name's Amsterdam."

"Panther."

"I said *stop it*!"

The snake stopped squirming, because the gorilla was ready to choke it to death.

"Don't kill it."

"I won't. But, I can. Say, aren't you a cat?"

"Yes."

"A big one."

"Yes."

"Not a lion."

"No."

"Cheetah? No way. You don't sound quick."

What the heck?

"You're a jaguar."

"Took you long enough." *Why?*

"So, what's your name?"

"Panther."

"You're a black jaguar---a *panther*. I get it."

"Fine."

"But, what is your name, dude?"

"I'm 'Panther'."

"I've got that, you ninny!"

Grrrrrrrr … "My name is Panther."

"You're not funny."

"Not usually."

"I don't get it."

"I'm *Panther*."

"Yeah, you're a jaguar."

"Whatever."

"You're not going to tell me your name."

"No."

"Fine."

"Fine."

"I don't care."

"Neither do I."

Amsterdam used his left paw to feel along a tree trunk on his left. He sat down, the huge serpent still in his right paw.

"Are you blind?" asked Panther.

"Indeed, I am."

The big cat suddenly felt really stupid.

"I'm sorry."

"'Bout what? So ... your name is ...?"

"Panther."

"Still not funny."

"Not tomorrow, either."

The drenching downpour, cold as it was, had slowed to a moderate rain, but it was hard to tell whether or not in the jungle if the lighter, smaller drops coming down were residue from the trees, so many trees, many limbs and branches, big leaves, plenty of pitter patter everywhere; it might "rain" for another hour or two, all of it canopy or tree-top residual.

The snake seemed resigned to its fate. It remained limp, if only because it could barely breathe.

"Please let me go," she said.

"Why should I?"

"What's your name?" said Panther.

"What's *yours*?" said Amsterdam, eyeing the big cat again, but not really; he'd cocked his big head in Panther's direction; however he was *visionary*, he had no vision.

"I'm Naja," said the snake.

"Panther."

"I don't think the snake has a sense of humor, either, jaguar."

"Give me a break, will you, fella'?"

"Please let me go," said the snake.

"You see," said Amsterdam, directing his attention to the snake, who could see, "panther or jaguar is a big cat, that's a wild animal, that's him, but he won't tell us who he is---frustrating."

"Let the snake go," said the big cat, who just shook his head and sighed.

"It's Naja," she said.

"You see, *she* has a name---*I've* a name!" said the blind gorilla, as he dropped the huge snake on the floor of the jungle. She gasped for air, lying flat on the terrain, not moving; regaining her bearings. "But, I like ya', anyway."

"You talking to me?"

"Yeah, and hopefully---" and he pointed at his own blind eyes with his huge paws---"I'm looking in your direction, as well."

"My *name* is *Panther*!"

"O.K., no name, forget it then---I still like ya', buddy!" Then it dawned on him. "Wait, you are a panther, a jaguar, whatever---"

"Yes."

"---and your name follows your species---Panther the black panther, actually a jaguar---*Wowwwwwww* ..."

"Yes."

"That's screwy, dude."

"No shit."

The big ape "looked" at the snake on the ground. "Naja's a pretty name," said Amsterdam, then cocked his head in Panther's direction again---"You *can't* be called what you are, dude!"

"Why *not*??"

"Because, it's not right."

"That makes so much sense in the jungle."

"Indeed, it doesn't."

"Panther is a panther," said Naja, as she regained her wind. "What's the big deal?"

"What are you?" said the cat to the snake.

"Egyptian Spitting Cobra."

"That sounds horrible!" said Amsterdam.

"Only when I'm hunting, dude!"

"Excuse me?"

"I spit when I hunt so I can eat."

"That's horrible."

"'Horrible'?! A gorilla's not exactly a beauty pageant contestant!"

"I'm actually a black jaguar," said Panther rather belatedly. "That gets lost in the translation." Perhaps, no translating was necessary at this point.

"I meant that you spit venom," said Amsterdam. "Not how you look."

"How'd *you* get here?"

"How'd *you* get here?"

"How'd *you* get here?"

All three stared quizzically at each other---well, again, Amsterdam could not, so there was *that* matter. Plus, no more translating ... Whatever. *Grrrrr* ...

"Transported to be sold," said Panther. "The truck crashed on the way. A squirrel saved me."

"What?!" said Amsterdam and Naja.

"Never mind!" said the big cat. "You've a tough enough time with my name!"

"Transported to be sold and cut up for decoration and delicacy," said Naja, who was still staring at the jaguar. Maybe, she thought he was cute. "I escaped. I don't remember how. I was drugged."

"Transported and experimented with here and tortured and I don't want to talk about it anymore," said Amsterdam.

Panther chuckled. He considered the irony.

They went silent. Raindrops continued to fall, regardless of their origin, from the canopies or the clouds. The trees and animals don't care, as long as they're able to receive.

The silence continued.

"How'd you escape??" they asked at once. All three then laughed. Naja might've giggled, too. She curled up in a ball, a bit more comfortable.

"Panther, what's your name?" said Amsterdam.

"It's 'Panther'---What's yours?" said the cobra to the gorilla.

"Amsterdam."

"Good," said Naja. "Panther and Amsterdam, now you know each other and me, Naja, and I know you two, too."

They went silent again. In the distance, a gator grunted in watery pleasure, probably Roberts in one of his canals. Sound travels like it's supposed to.

Clouds broke up and the moon shone through, still floating as its perceptual self.

"So, Panther," said Naja, "You're a black jaguar?"

"Yes." *Thank you*, thought Panther. *He's confused enough as it is*. Amsterdam could reply with, *It's not 'confusion', it's common-sense.*

"How did you lose your sight?" said the cobra. She had a nice voice, for a snake, sounding a lot like … like, *my former mate*. Ummm … *She's a snake, dude.* The moon had taken over, imbedding crazier thoughts into the living. Panther decided it was time to move along.

It was night. A red-tail hawk landed on an oak branch, not far from the big cat's current limb of snooze. (He was not there right now, but would be whenever he chose.)

Over there, near a small bog that was connected to the swamp (all the bogs around here are), Brian and Nathaniel landed on a dead log. They always land on a dead log. (Some animals have a thing for dead logs.) Then again, this raven and crow were best friends. Whichever bird decided to land on said dead log, the other followed.

Panther stopped in his tracks.

"Why are you letting her live?" said Elaine, who knew just a bit---a *lot* of bit---about hunting, if not swallowing whole like a poisonous or constrictor serpent, her prey. She'd landed on the log, too. How nice.

"We let *you* live," said Panther.

"We let *you* live."

"*You* didn't have a choice."

"Where'd the snake come from?" said Nathaniel, who then picked at the log with his beak, checking for grubs to eat.

"Isn't one snake enough?" said Brian. Panther figured he was referring to Robert the reticulated python.

"Why don't you guys go pick on the pigeons?" said the big cat.

"You have pigeons here?" said Amsterdam, who was "moving along", too. "Yuck, they're *filthy* beasts."

"They taste like caca, too," reflected Elaine as she flapped her wings.

The raindrops still fell as residue from whatever height, leaves, twigs. The sky: So many stars. The daily one or two thunderstorms do what they're supposed to do: Cleanse and feed. But, soon, the moisture on the turf and waterways would evaporate and the sky-view dissipate with humidity, a new camouflage of mist which started the whole process again for tomorrow and more storminess.

Panther looked at the cobra.

"I don't suppose you could tell me why you attacked me," he said.

"I'll tell you why I attacked you if you tell me why you're called 'Panther'."

Panther slapped his left paw over his eyes.

"When you *are* one," said Amsterdam.

"Ooooh," said Brian, "I wouldn't go there if I were you."

"Crikey!" cried Panther.

"He's very sensitive about that," said Elaine, who was trying to forget about those pigeons---they tasted *yucky*.

"Yeah, it's kinda' a sore subject," said Nathaniel, who swallowed a few grubs.

"Dude, that's disgusting," said Brian.

"I'm a bird!"

"Yeah, but there's better meat out there---you know?"

"Panther's *Panther* because he is," said Elaine.

The big cat slapped his *right* paw over his face. Darkness: here. He was hungry and needed to hunt.

"That's just *wrong*," said Amsterdam. He couldn't see a thing anymore, but he was very observant, anyway---excellent hearing and sense of smell, taste, and touch.

Nothing was wrong with a jaguar having the name Panther.

"I'm a black jaguar, by genus," said Panther. *Why'd I say that?! Who cares??*

"A *what*?"

"I'm in the jaguar family, if only by coloring."

"I don't understand," said the gorilla.

"The reason I went after you, as you stepped on my tail and I thought you were going to kill and eat me," said Naja.

Panther looked dumbfounded. He didn't remember stepping on a snake. Then again, it had been raining and the senses can fail you in inclement weather. That's why he never comes down from his tree when the weather goes bad. Don't want to be accused of stepping on anything dangerous.

"I don't remember what my real name is," said Panther. "I never saw my parents. I was taken as a cub in Brazil and lived with humans for several years."

"Why *Panther*?" said Amsterdam.

"Does it matter?"

"No. Sorry."

"It matters more that you're blind. My name isn't a big deal. Your blindness is."

"I don't remember having eyesight." He reached out and grabbed the log Nathaniel and Brian were perched on. "But, I can find things. And my hearing is excellent." The log shifted with the gorilla's grip.

"I don't doubt that."

"Should we move?" Nathaniel asked. Brian shook his head. Amsterdam released his grip.

"How'd you get here, Panther?"

"I was sold to a zoo here and shipped from Brazil. The truck carrying me crashed and with the help of Butts the squirrel managed to get away shaken but uninjured and survive."

"I was a lab rat in a university as a youngster and blinded by alcohol."

"How's that?"

"Some human decided to get me drunk on grain alcohol and, well, you don't do that with humans, either."

"Bad batch."

"I guess so."

"I saw the humans drink that stuff in South America. Fortunately, they liked it too much to try sharing it with the animals."

"I was flushed down a toilet," said Naja. "They didn't realize that exotic species, especially snakes, means 'poisonous'."

"O.K., well, we've got lousy beginnings. But, here we are."

"I'm exhausted; I've been travelling from the north since yesterday. Do you mind if I stick around a bit and get some sleep?" She was directing this question to Panther. To her thinking, he was in charge. She was right to think that way.

"How 'bout if you stick around longer than 'a bit' and just don't eat anyone?"

"Thank you."

"What about me? said Amsterdam. "I won't cause any trouble."

"Stick around," said Panther.

"Where do you hunt, Panther?"

"Around the swamp; sometimes, I fish in it."

"Can I *hunt* there, as well?"

"Yeah, I doubt we eat the same things."

"I eat berries," said the gorilla. "Lots of fruit---leaves and twigs, too."

"Well, then, you'll never be sober around here."

"Lotta' rotting fruit here?"

"And then some."

"Any of them taste like whiskey?"

"What is that?"

"Humans drink it."

"You've had it?"

"And then some, but my whiskey comes from the fruits, but I forget which ones cure like that."

"There are so many fruits around. I'm sure you'll find that flavor."

"Or impact."

"Why are you being so nice to a huge, carnivorous man-eater?" said Elaine as she flapped her wings; *always with the wings---Just take off, will ya'*? Panther shook his head with mindful admonition.

"I don't eat meat, ma'am," said Amsterdam. "You may have me confused with chimpanzees---they eat meat from time to time."

"I eat meat from time to time," said Nathaniel.

"Me, too," said Brian.

"Gotta' love those fast-food leftovers."

"Me, too."

Panther considered what they were saying. He couldn't see himself in a parking lot raiding leftover fast-food boxes and wraps. He'd end up looking and acting … like the pigeons? No way.

"You two flying over the suburb?" he asked.

"Only in the middle of the night when we can't sleep," said Brian.

"He snores," said Nathaniel. "I can't sleep when that happens."

"I also fart."

"Me, too."

"Maybe you should try separate branches," said Amsterdam.

Panther sighed. He looked at Amsterdam, then at Naja.

He said to the gorilla, "How did you get here?"

"Walked. But, I could smell the fermentation from miles away. That made it easier to locate this place."

"Well, you're welcome to stay here."

"Just stay off your limb."

"I don't have a 'limb'. Usually, the tree I'm closest to at the time exhaustion overtakes suffices."

"Pretty simple," said Naja, who was already nodding off where she lay curled up.

"Meanwhile, I'm hungry. Birds: Don't follow me."

"We won't," said Elaine.

"Not," said Brian.

"Uh uh," said Nathaniel.

Chapter 4: Kittay

Animals stood and sat in the clearing, and several perched or hung on a branch or limb, depending on the size of their paws and claws and strength and tensility of their tails.

Chimp hung from a branch like a primate should. He used the opposable thumb of his right hand to assist the other four fingers in the endeavor; not an exercise, just hanging out.

Emily the angora cat, who hung with Chimp, sat on the branch above and to the right. She couldn't be alongside; otherwise she'd be hanging, too, and cats do not prefer that approach to hanging out, by themselves or with others. Now: She had a better view of the mystery out there about 100 feet away.

William the pygmy tarsier leapt from Seysew's head where he'd left some pellets behind in his haste to make waste and clung to a twig about five inches long, about his length, and because he weighed so little, about three ounces, it appeared that the twig had suddenly grown a brown and black leaf with eyes so big, so he could see at night, and it wasn't nighttime, so he didn't need his pupils to be so big in the daytime to know, to see a large and vague shape looming in the dusk, out there, about 100 feet away.

The tiny primate clung to "his" twig, looking like a large-enough leaf, vibrating ever slightly with his grab and grip, perhaps with excitement, anticipation; he could've used his tensile tail instead. Perhaps, when he has a chunk of mango, he'd use his tail to hang out upside down, gripping the juicy fruit in his paws and chomping away, a position a pygmy tarsier can appreciate.

There were other animals in the clearing, which Seysew's size and bulk tried to overwhelm but not quite. Animals were foraging---squirrels, raccoons, chipmunks, a panda bear, wolverine, and so many pigeons flying overhead and landing in the surrounding trees.

The pigeons made everyone nervous because they shit so much; when they did, it was epic. The rest of the clearing clan looked up to make sure there were no more pigeons up there swirling around because you never knew where and when they might drop their shit, or shed their droppings, dribble their doo doo; their haste does leave waste. The pigeons' helter skelter walk and flight are always about how unpredictable they are when leaving their crap behind, from their behinds.

"Who's got the balls to find out who it is?" said William, who had a pretty big voice, however un-scary (Look how *small* the dude is!) for five ounces ... four ... three ... stop.

"What it is ..." said Butts, who sat on a branch that ended in leafy twigs and grew ahead of a limb alongside several other branches with leafy twigs.   Well, not his balls, either.

Chipmunk sat on another branch---well, a twig, let's not get carried away---and surveyed the looming mystery as the others did and provided the profundity. (Not his balls, either.)

"Who gets to investigate?"

"You mean, 'Seysew, go check it out,'" said Seysew.

"It might come to us," said William.

"Chipmunk?" said Butts.

"*Whaaaat?*"

"Climb higher."

"*Whyyyyyy?*"

"Because I'll eat you if you don't," said Panther. He had snuck in, with stealth as he does, creeping along the jungle floor. Nobody had heard him. "I'm just kidding. But, climb higher. You'll make the squirrel feel important because somebody listened to him."

"Big guy," said the squirrel. "I really don't need your wit."

"I don't think he was trying to be witty, Butts," said Jamie. She was on Seysew's left flank, and Panther had moved up on the pachyderm's right. Raccoons weren't known for stealth or being creepy. No, they were noted for knocking over garbage cans.

There was the subtlest of movement in the distance, a shift of a paw. Panther noticed. He froze. The others noticed that Panther noticed and *they* froze.

Butts finished crunching an acorn and swallowed with a gulp. He could see a tail, black, way out there. He shook his head and crouched on the branch. His tail did not move. Chipmunk did the same on his twig, except he hadn't been masticating a nut. William peed and it dribbled to the ground where it landed on some ants.

"*Jackass!*" they all yelled. But, they're such small critters. No one can hear them more than a few feet away, several yards, whatever, not much.

"Was that necessary?" said Seysew out the side of her mouth. Whether she was admonishing William or the ants or both, it was hard to tell.

Chimp and Emily remained motionless, as were the others.

There was no breeze. It was hot and humid. A jungle is supposed to be. Otherwise, no animal made a sound; they sensed danger.

A branch snapped. A shifting of leaves, then a small tree broke in half and the broken and leafy upper portion, about 10 feet long, was thrown across the clearing and high over Seysew's head.

Amsterdam landed with a thud in front of Seysew, facing toward the mysterious beast 100 feet away. He had Naja around his neck.

"I know a gator and python who are close like that," said William.

"'The eagle has landed,'" said Panther.

"Not an eagle, big guy," said Butts.

"Never mind."

A shadow shifted in the distance, big enough to reflect off the nearest tree trunks and rocks; the beast must have leapt high enough, angle of the Earth and waning sun, and geometry. There was no flight, no silhouette against the sky; it couldn't have been a pterodactyl.

"Yeah?"

"Never mind on that climb."

"I already did." Then he left some pellets, which fell down, bouncing off twigs and landed on the ground ... *tiff* *tiff* *tiff* ...

"Oh."

"See anything, Seysew?" said Panther.

"No. You know what or who it is?"

"No."

"Yes," said Jamie.

Panther glanced under the elephant toward the lady raccoon.

"How so?"

"I think you know who."

"How so?"

"I'm a woman. I know."

"I can't dispute the first part."

"A woman always knows."

"Who or what do you think that I think it is?"

"We'll know soon enough."

"Meanwhile, back at the ranch," said Amsterdam as he sniffed the air.

"There's no ranch around here," said Butts.

"Never mind."

"I'll explain it you squirrel, sometime," said Chimp.

"Does that snake on your neck ever talk?" said Chipmunk.

"When spoken to," said Amsterdam.

"Hello, snake," said Butts.

"Hello," said Naja.

"It's 'Naja,'" said the gorilla.

"Hello, Naja," said the squirrel.

"Hello."

"I guess you could swallow me and others here, whole."

"He's Butts," said Panther. "Or, 'squirrel', or 'idiot'---take your pick."

"Hello, 'Butts,'" said Naja. Then, to Panther, "Why are you so mean?"

"Because I can be."

"Grumpy, too," said Jamie.

"Yeah, you can call me Panther, Big Cat, Big Guy, Grumpy, Mean …"

"*Jackass* …" said Butts.

"That, too."

Amsterdam maneuvered with his reptilian neck-wrap counter-clockwise around Seysew, at times tapping the pachyderm with his left paw to mark his path; whether it was a dance or not, it was hard to tell.

Naja's forked tongue worked in unison to guide him as he found himself in front of a crouching Panther. The blind gorilla sat and faced the big cat, or "Jackass", while the Egyptian spitting cobra regarded the jaguar with caution, her upright and flanged neck on alert and open. It's what cobras do.

"Chill," said the big cat.

"Oh, my," said Jamie as she trundled around from the other side.

"Naja, knock it off!" said Amsterdam.

"You've nothing to prove to me," said Panther, "and I might just eat you."

"Do you have any idea who that was, Panther?" said Jamie.

"It was a kitty cat," said Amsterdam.

"How would you know?"

Panther remained quiet, having "dealt" with Naja and perhaps wrong about her aggressiveness and character.

He was wrong, on both counts.

"It's not a 'kitty cat,'" said the jaguar.

He was wrong about that.

"Sure, it is," said the gorilla. "It's one of your kind."

"*That's* not a *kitty cat*!"

Right about that.

"No," said Emily, "I'm a kitty cat. She was *much much* bigger."

"'She'?"

"'She.'"

They all looked at Panther.

"Something they should know?" said Amsterdam.

"'They'?" said Jamie.

"Well, I'm just visiting."

"No, you're not," said Emily. "You're here. If you leave, then you were 'visiting.'"

"Well put," said Chimp.

"I'm not leaving unless you want me to," said the gorilla.

"You're staying," said Panther.

"Please," said Naja.

"Yeah, you, too---Didn't we already establish this?"

"Is it her?" said Jamie. The question was directed at Panther.

"What---How do I know?"

"You know."

"It isn't an elephant," said Seysew.

"It isn't a chipmunk," said Chipmunk.

"It isn't a chimpanzee, or a monkey---"

"Nor an orangutan, baboon, or gorilla," said Amsterdam.

"---Not a spider or howler or rhesus," finished Chimp.

"Not a pygmy tarsier," said William.

"Much bigger than me," said Emily.

"Pygmy tarsier?" said Amsterdam.

"Yeah, we have one of those," said Panther.

"Tiny bastard," said Chimp.

"Hey!" said William.

They all stared at him.

"You're right."

"Not a squirrel, either," said Butts.

"Raccoons are much more aggressive," said Jamie. "No stealth."

"Yeah, but you're a wimp compared to Cindy."

"I don't need to be a wolverine, dear. I'm tough enough."

"True," said Panther. "I'll see you later." The big cat scampered off, a whisper between the trees, under the branches, barely a leaf shifting in his wake---stealth and wraith-like.

"Not a wolverine, either," said Cindy.

"Could be," said Emily. "You might be mean enough."

"I'm so bad."

"Not like the jaguar," said Amsterdam.

"Is it time to get drunk?" said William.

"Is that all you ever think about---rotting fruit?!" said Seysew.

"I've seen you eat your share of fermentation," said Jamie.

"You calling me a lush?!"

"You calling William a lush??"

"I'm a lush," said Jamie. "I guess."

"Me, too," said Chipmunk.

"Here, here," said Cindy.

"Yo," said Chimp.

"I'm blind, but not from drinking," said Amsterdam. "But, I can go for some of that 'fermentation.'"

"Same here," said Nathaniel.

"Yup," said Brian.

"Blackberries, strawberries, raspberries, blueberries … *Yeah*, baby!" exclaimed Emily.

"What about you, jaguar?" said Elaine as she flew over, sounding the Doppler again.

"Not here," said Jamie. "But, he's a lush, too."

"You dare to speak for him?!" said Amsterdam, probably in a mocking tone.

"Eh."

"Fruit is good for you," said Rachel, "no matter its aging."

"Not me," said Roberts.

"You're full of crap," said Robert.

"But, not from Happy Hour … I made a joke, dude."

"You eat the mangos over near the swamp … dude."

"*Shhhhhhh ...*"

"I like my mangos," said William.

"I'd like to try some," said Naja.

"Just don't eat me in the process, you beautiful thing."

"Thank you ... and I won't ... eat you."

"How could you tell?" said Amsterdam. "He's so small, like an acorn."

"For a blind and hairy beast," said William, "You know so much."

"They're bigger than you are," said Chimp as he hopped off of Seysew. Emily climbed down after him.

"Yeah, but they're good for me---especially when they're overripe."

"You're so loveable," said Jamie, with a smile.

"Thank you." William smiled back. He remained hanging by his tail, mango juice all over his face. He might be the biggest and smallest lush of them all.

"Do you think we should follow Panther?" said Seysew.

"I'm always following him," said Amsterdam. "It's what I do."

"Why would you do that?" said Butts.

"Better him than you," said Chipmunk. "He's bigger."

"Why do you follow him?" said Jamie.

"Well, he's not omnipotent," said the gorilla. "He bleeds like the rest of us."

"I don't think he'd appreciate that you follow him," said Seysew.

"I admire him and he admires me. Can any of you say that with conviction?"

"I think we all can," said Jamie.

"Not if you need to come to his rescue."

"Maybe not," said Butts.

"Since when has the jungle become so dangerous that Panther would need someone to watch *his* back?" said Seysew.

"Since just about every beast on this planet seems to be finding their way here."

"I can protect him, too."

"You're a woman," said Amsterdam. "I don't think he responds well to that."

"He doesn't have a choice, Amsterdam."

"True. I guess. Well, I'm going to meander. Naja?"

The cobra unfurled and slithered or slunk along the floor of the jungle.

"He'll move too quick and that upsets my stomach," said Naja.

"I wouldn't want you wrapped around me, either," said Rachel.

"I don't understand these attractions," said Chimp. "Animals."

"Look in a wading pool," said Cindy. "See yourself."

"Is it Happy Hour, yet?"

"You'rrrre ... kidding," said Emily.

"I think I'm still digesting," said William.

"No, you just started early," said Rachel.

"So?" said Chimp. "Why can't I?"

Panther crouched on a limb and scrutinized the forest, shifting his green eyes left to right, and right to left.

Dusk was evident in the shadows up high, 50 feet or more up in the loftier branches, because the sun didn't give a crap---didn't do much reaching to the forest floor, no matter the time of day or time of year.

In the summer, right now, the sun's rays spent a few hours reaching in, poking, squeezing and stretching to the jungle's core, allowing new shoots, sprouts of baby trees to reach out and get their quantified if short-lived share of daily sun---and that isn't much, for the pines and bushes and ferns grab their share, horde down low; even the long grass is a bully for sunlight, and it is a battle, a war for nourishment from the tundra to about 10 to 15 feet up.

Panther waited. He stayed on the turf, amongst the detritus, crouched low, enveloped by long grass, alert; his eyes shut allowing the sounds of the jungle to reach him, soak in, remind him of days in his youth within thicker and denser jungle than this, where there were so many snakes, big ones, constrictors, huge beasts everywhere like Robert, and many other jaguars and primates and abundant fish of all sizes---some as big and more dangerous than the land beasts---and this area where he lived now, near the Florida Bay and the thunderstorms that developed over the Florida Keys and stacked up, cumulonimbus over the Bay. They seemed to sit there, like in his youth, thousands of feet high, miles thick and---

"I thought you might want some company."

"No."

"Well, I'm here anyway."

"You can leave."

"It's a hobby of mine: covering friends' backs."

"I'm not your friend."

"You don't have a choice, cat---I'm here."

"You can't see."

"Yes. I can, in my mind's eye."

"Really?"

Panther climbed an elm and reached the lowest limb and crouched.

"I would go higher if I were you. That way she can't sneak down from above. Cats are good climbers. But, I'm guessing *you* already knew that ... cat."

"Who's 'she'?"

"Me," said a voice that crouched alongside Amsterdam's right hip.

How did he not smell her or hear her and the blind ape did? He's concentrating too much on potential trouble. *Well, she's trouble, too. ... Never mind.*

"I knew you were there the whole time," said the gorilla.

"I just *got* here."

"You know what I mean."

Panther looked over his left shoulder and down and slapped his right paw over his eyes. It could've been his left paw, but his right was quicker, this time. Never mind.

"Such stealth-recognizance on your part," said the voice to Panther.

"I knew you were there, too."

"No, you didn't."

"What do you want, Kittay?"

"Hi, I'm Amsterdam," said Amsterdam. He glanced in her direction, unseeing but seeing all. Well, maybe not this time. (Never mind.)

"I know."

"Figures. You've been sneaking around, yeah? Listening in."

"She's always been crafty," said Panther.

"You mean devious," said Kittay.

"Not quite the word."

"Not grumpy like you."

"Why are you here?"

"She missed you, cat," said Amsterdam.

"Nope."

"Yep."

"Shut up, Amsterdam," said Kittay.

"Don't tell him to 'shut up,'" said Panther. "He's been watching my back, usually with a cobra around his neck."

"Watching your back whether you like it or not," said the silverback. "It's what I do for friends."

"Gee, maybe I can be your friend and you can watch my back, too," said Kittay.

"Sure, I can do that."

"*Why* are you here?!"

"Don't be grumpy," said Kittay.

"Yeah, don't be grumpy, pinhead," said the ape.

"'Pinhead'?! I *like* that."

"I don't," said Panther.

"So … um … Why are you here?" said Amsterdam. "Anyone else out there curious besides *Pinhead* and I---?"

"Stop with the 'pinhead'---!"

"Cat!"

"---That's *better*!"

"I'm *here*," said the lady panther, "because your kids are grown and on their own---"

"And she missed you."

"---*Maybe*."

"*Women*!" said Panther.

"Yeah, I'll agree with *that*---*Women*!" said the gorilla.

A red-tail hawk named Elaine came flying overhead, swooped low and picked a poisonous asp off the ground nearby and flew off, the viper struggling uselessly in the raptor's strong claws' grip. She'd rip the head off later with her lightning-quick beak and sharp talons.

"I'm glad Naja wasn't here," said Amsterdam. "She might not have appreciated that."

"If she had been, she wouldn't be here now," said Panther.

"She's a bit bigger than that asp. She would've proved a tough haul."

"Let's go talk somewhere," said Kittay.

"I thought I told you to hunt in or near the *swamp*!" yelled Panther, looking up to the sky.

"Big cat?" said the silverback.

"Yeah?"

"Who wants an asp around?"

"That's not nice," said Kittay.

"That sounds familiar, hmmm," said the big cat. "Rules are rules, ape. We abide, or there is anarchy."

"O.K."

"Never mind."

Panther hadn't moved from the limb, still staring out into the wilderness, with no apparent reason other than that he could.

"You were talking to me?"

"Any other jaguar here besides you and I?"

"It's getting late, isn't it?" said Amsterdam.

"Aren't you supposed to be watching my back, primate?"

"'Primate'? Aren't you the sly one."

"A very large primate---"

"And you're a very big kitty."

"---*Enough*," said Kittay.

Amsterdam glanced in her direction, his acute sense of hearing gathering in her position, now moving. His sense of smell was pretty acute, too.

"Well, now," he said.

"She's a woman---"

"Moody."

"---In charge."

Overhead, two birds came swooping in from the direction of the sun, in silhouette, one larger than the other. They landed on a branch above Panther, who was about ready to disembark and follow his mate---current, former, future ... he knew there was a *former* in there, but otherwise he really had no idea.

The silverback "looked" up.

"Where you two go, the slovenly ones are sure to follow," he said.

"Like, you leave nothing for them to scavenge, Panther?" said Brian the raven.

"Remember, pigeons eat *anything*, carrion-face," said Nathaniel the crow.

"I guess I resemble that remark," said the big cat.

Shhhhhh ... There they were (*ahhhh*, whose fault it is) flying in no formation whatsoever or noticeable, haphazard, full of shit (always, it seems), ready to dump (always, it seems) ---

Where are they going to land?!

Please, not here!

Not there!

---"Are you coming or not?" said Kittay.

"Do you have any idea what we're under?" Panther said toward the sky.

"What's their act?" said Amsterdam.

"Shit. Lots of it."

"They didn't follow us," said Nathaniel.

"We don't really know that, do we?" said Brian.

"You guys fly in!" shouted Panther as he skedaddled, "and these flying vermin follow!"

"That's not always true, Panther!" yelled Brian.

"All of you poop from the air, don't you?" said Amsterdam. "*Birds.*"

The pigeons … hundreds, thousands, more than before, perhaps too many to count, kept flying, if that's what you'd calling *flying*---so many of them managed to maneuver between and under low-lying branches, and no one was out of harm's way---

Not even themselves …

---"No, this way---*this* way!" yelled out Panther in the distance, shifting left to right, Doppler moving away, follow that freight train into the dusk.

"They really do stink, don't they?" said Amsterdam, as he readied himself to bolt. Where? Follow the big cat? Did he know? They're pigeons! Run for your lives!!

"Stay away from this branch!" yelled Nathaniel.

"Ditto!" screamed Brian.

So many of the winged caca-heads were close enough to *that* branch and so many others.

Like locusts, they swarmed everywhere, not stopping, not alighting, not headed for a roost, not yet. They really didn't know what they were doing, where they were going, where they were; they made the dodo bird look smart.

The dodo didn't take up airspace and foul the atmosphere.

Maybe they had Happy Hour, too.

Rotting fruit then and now.

Chapter 5: Benja

The pigeons just wanted to fly. Sometimes, even the not-so-smart just wanna' fly. Who knows what the dodo thought? Maybe they didn't crap at random like the pigeons.

Does anyone crap at random like the pigeons? All that junk food they scavenged from the college campus and the encroaching suburbs---well, it had to go somewhere.

Panther followed after Kittay and thought, *I can't keep those damn birds from crappin' over the jungle.* That thought, innocuous as it was, came and went as fast as the red-tail hawk's pounce. That's fast.

Kittay was setting a fast pace, and Panther struggled to keep up. He didn't stop to wonder what the hurry was. If he stopped, he'd have been further behind and in trouble for it. It was possible she'd forgiven him for staying with the other animals, remaining their guardian instead of asking about making a new territory with her. He'd also figured that their kids were full grown and somewhere else---or they could be dead.

It all seemed so long ago. Well, so was Brazil, and that was longer than "long ago."

O.K., she came back because she was all alone. Panther shook his head at this thought. One other: *She has another mate.*

No. She wouldn't've come. It can't be that. Could it? Panther shook his head again and sped up, closing the gap between his former mate and himself.

She's gotta' have a mate---that's what she's supposed to do---stupid!!

What horses do he did: he galloped and now he caught up to her. A lightning bolt flashed in the distance near the top of the horizon and ... no thunder, not yet ... the storm was somewhere else.

Wait ... An off-white and speckled-gray thunderhead came rushing through the trees, a swirling billowing mass of--- What?!?! Birds???

Yes, pigeons. But, normally these animals---and the caste of mammals and those *humans* within that caste, hangin', sittin', stoopin', *stooopid*, fartin' around on the animal family tree---were cast like outcasts in grayish white coats, or some such hue or splatter (pattern ... or, shit). This thunderstorm of birds in black, brown, dark green, and various striations of gray and puce ... *gag* ... through the trees.

No, this thunder-mosh was grayish-white and fluttering, bumping, careening along, seemingly having a gay old time ... that's the 1890's style of gay, before the world of words got skewered in the 20th Century, and we're digressing here a bit---

Whooooshhh!! Overhead and gone and ... *not poopin'?!?!*

Push!! Panther was slammed sideways about 20 feet, tumbling, scraping, yowling---**Roaring!!**

What the ... *much* bigger than he. Orange and white coat, *thick* coat and body long as a cut limb from a powerful kapok tree.

Kittay slithered out to the right side, the other *much* bigger cat's left.

"He remembers you!" she cried.

"New mate?" Panther shook his head after the blind-slide.

"C'mon, you know I only have eyes for your size, big boy."

"Oh." He slapped his left paw over his left eye and sat. "You have such a way with the gab, babe."

"So do you, as in 'new mate'; that was so witty ... quick ... sloppy ... *stupid*."

"You two," said the much bigger and very huge cat-beast, "Do you ever shut up?"

"Who ... *are* you?" said Panther, suddenly glancing over to stare at the big boy---*bigger* boy.

"I am Benja," said he as he pounded his chest with a huge right paw.

"You got indigestion?"

"Panther!" said Kittay.

"I am a Bengal tiger," said Benja. "I was born in Borneo and swept off to Mongolia to grow---so big---*too* big!"

"You said it," said the smaller big cat. "Do you know Amsterdam?"

"'Am-tur-dummy'?"

"Careful, he might out-weigh you, fatso."

"If I am 'fatso' … (hesitates) … I am *not* *pound* *pound* … (hesitates) … Then, what is he?"

"*Really* fat---"

"*Panther!!*"

"---so … *So*, what did you say about a zoo?"

"What zoo?"

"Zoo!"

Kittay was giggling and moved closer to Panther.

"Oh, yeah---Zoo! I was in one."

"I almost was---just *missed*, dammit'!!" The jaguar pounded his chest with his left paw, pounded hard to emphasize two differences in these big and biggest puddy tats. He wasn't sure if the Bengal … via Borneo … via Mongolia … Now, here?! It's so hot, here!

"You break a nail doing that? You hit so hard, I might play with you---you're so *mean*-sounding."

Panther winced. It had hurt but he covered up in a manly way---he farted. Things might now die.

"What am I *doing* here?!" said Kittay, who scrunched up her nose.

"That's how you fart, little kitty? Let me show you how." Benja pointed his butt cheeks skyward, or at least 45 degrees, his broad long tail, too, and let go. The small bamboo forest behind lit up in unison courtesy of the liquid-heated fart from the Bengal-raised-in-Mongolia's raised behind and burned and flew off as ashes.

Really? Yes.

So, the bamboo was really dry; usually is.

Not sure about that.

"That was faked, c'mon," said Kittay. She thought she might have tears, a reaction to the odor.

"No," said Panther, who felt an alert in his soul. "That was real, and he's the champ of the gas games. No one out-farts this cat---not *any* other big cat or gorilla or elephant or python or pygmy tarsier or school of piranha. He's the hot-wet and stinkiest methane bomber of them all."

"Thank you," said the Bengal.

"By the way, bamboo burns easily, but still …"

"How … *exciting* for you," said the raccoon. She was referring to the fart king … maybe … yeah … not sure.

Panther glared over at his former mate … current … future … not sure.

"More exciting than sitting, crouching---"

"slouching"

"---*crouching* on the limb looking out over the jungle vigilant for animals whom he *does* call his friends"; much more consistent than Kittay appeared to ever have been with him. Of course, she must've thought he did it on purpose when first the land baron/oil magnate took him then sold him to a bigger idiot (about the same size idiot) who sold him to a zoo contractor (another one … idiot) and then that crash-and-rescue.

"Benja?" said Panther.

"Yes, little kitty?"

"Knock that off!!"

"Well, you're a little pussy cat to me."

"You're calling me a ...?"

Sigh

"Big kitty?" continued Panther.

"Yes, little kitty?"

"Do you care what she thinks?" and he pointed at Kittay, his eyes shut tight.

"No, she's even teenier than you."

Teenier?!

"Thanks for noticing," said Kittay.

"Why is she here?" said Panther.

"I don't know," said Benja. "She's like lampreys on a shark: can't get rid of her."

"You feel the same way."

"All the time."

Kittay sighed.

"You remember Pantherville in Brazil?"

"Yeah, I used to live there. Guy real dickhead, but keep plenty of big cats, other Bengals, some bigger than me, plenty of water buffalo meat, though, always fresh, must've paid lots for that."

"Yeah, lots of meat in Pantherville." Panther licked his lips.

"You never told me this," said Kittay.

"Before you. Before a lot. Right after I was born. Everyone brought there as cubs. We were all rescue---from fires and being alone. No dads or moms.

"You were there, little kitty---?"

"It's *Panther*!"

"How is it your name is the same as what you are?"

"Well---*Damn*! At least you get it ... quicker than most!"

"Why??"

"'Why'?!"

"Yeah, why are you a panther and named the same?"

"Actually ... I'm a jaguar." Panther sniffed.

"No, you're a little---*echem*---no one names their cub like that."

"My parents did."

The big Bengal stared.

"And I'm not a little ... *whatever!*"

"O.K. O.K. ... *Panther!* Benja kinda' spat the name out. "Named after what you are---kinda' asinine."

"O.K."

"Ohhhh, gosh," said Kittay.

"You were there and his favorite. You weren't allowed to fight. He kept you close, like teddy-bear close."

"That's right," said the jaguar. "I remember."

"We used to laugh about that ... Ha ha ho ho."

"I would've torn you a new one, Benja. I was faster except for the cheetahs, but faster than you just not big like you. But, I would've torn off your face, just the same. He kept me close because of my temper. I never fought fair. He'd lose too much of his investment if he *didn't* keep me close. I *had* to be close. I fought like I was much bigger and sprinted like I was much smaller.

"You weighed about 350 back then."

"An anomaly."

"I weigh a lot more than 350."

"I don't care. I'd still tear your nostrils out."

"You're so mean."

"Thank you."

"He's so mean," said Kittay and giggled.

Benja and Panther glanced at each other: "Women."

"How'd you get here?" said Benja.

"We've all got stories."

"You know, it's really driving me nuts."

"What?"

"Your name."

"Panther."

"Your real name."

"*Again*?!?!"

"What you are is not a name, and I'm not called 'Tiger' because it is what I am, not who I am---so why should you be?"

"*Really*?!?!"

"Benja?" said Kittay.

"I'm not *Tiger*. I can't be *Tiger*. That's Tiger the tiger. I am that, not *who* that ... Is."

"*What*?!?!"

"I'm *Tiger*---No! I'm *not*! I have a *real* name!"

"Pinch me, I'll *show* you how real I am, fat cat!"

"What's your real name?"

"Benja?" sighed Kittay.

"Whatever."

"Why isn't it ... *Jaguar*?"

"*Panther*---stupid!!" Panther blew a raspberry. Panther never blows raspberries. He just did.

"'Panther---stupid'?"

"Knock that off, Benja---!"

"See? I have a name!"

"---I'm **Panther!!!**"

"Benja!!"

"Panther!!"

"Right!"

"Left!"

"I'm gonna' fart again!"

Kittay groaned.

"Be my guest, *jackass*!"

A flash of red and gray and silver swooped between and grabbed a field mouse or some such unlucky critter with a long tail and whiskers and flew off.

"What was that?!"

"I don't *know*!!"

Kittay sat off nearer the water. Where'd the water come from? Sky.

"Are we done with this?"

"Yeah. I'm exhausted."

"Don't you wish you could fly?"

"Not really. You?"

"Not really."

"You still gonna' fart?"

Kittay sighed.

"No."

"Good. You're loud."

"Any water buffalo around here?"

"I don't know. Everything else edible seems to be."

"I like fish, too."

"So do I."

"I weigh a lot more than you do."

"So what?"

"Right."

"Left."

Kittay rolled her lady jaguar eyes.

Nathaniel the crow and Brian the raven landed over near Kittay. She scooched further away. She didn't know them. They didn't know her. It's Pantherville. You will know each other if you wanna' stay.

Kittay: Stuck up? Nah. Yup. Maybe.

Benja and Panther witnessed her subtle maneuver.

Women.

"We're about to vacate this area, Benja."

"Why?"

"Just trust me. Go over there."

"I don't run from anyone."

"Just ... trust me on this." They scampered over *there*. "Do you do limbs?"

"Not usually."

"Can you climb?"

"Heck, yeah!"

"Do it. Trust me."

They leapt up a huge kapok tree, big enough for the both of them and a few other jaguars and tigers; with huge limbs, lots of leafy overhang---camouflage.

There was a rush, like the air was leaving the area, displacement, a vacuum, like a huge sucking sound; then animals with wings (called: birds ... sometimes, bats) and bunched together because, well, they know nothing else; they're here and moving fast and scattered everywhere, out-of-control, in flight but barely, looking to crash-land, guess they're not sure, not sure of anything, these birds---fly on by, everyone else, run and hide for cover, find a tree over there ... watch out for the big kitties ... "Benja!" "Panther!" ... **GRRRRRR!!** ... (Right) (Left) ... find another tree.

Whoooosh! All you need is that first *Whooosh* and there they are, again, here, what else but *Whooosh*. This time is not like the last few times---*this* time they're looking---leaving behind their troubles, so much trouble, so much ... waste ... this is *not* a false alarm.

"How'd you know?" said Benja, glancing, looking terrorized, not just fearful or scared because he never was. This was different. This was shit.

Panther had his paws up over his head and covering his ears.

"They fly with more purpose, like a straight line but probably not and we're hoping"---the smell---"ducking our heads."

"We're up on a limb, so what does it matter about ducking our heads? Shit lands where it does."

Millions ... must've been (noooo wayyy) ... Maybe not ... So many ... At least thousands (nope) ... O.K., hundreds. In front of them, the greens, browns, flowers, clean animal hair and fur, smooth feathers and bright round eyes meant for night-vision and hunting and so many pigeons about to ruin it all.

"They're taking a massive shit!" yelled Benja.

"*Leaving* a massive shit---!" yelled Panther.

"*Whatever*!!"

In front of them, it was beautiful, it was jungle, swamp, the bay beyond and the gulf, then an ocean, but behind these flying caca-heads---*eeeeeuuu* ...

"This is all about dumping?!?!" Benja: Incredulous.

"I feel better when I do!" said Panther. "I'm sure they do, too!"

"Well, so do I---but *this*?!?!"

"Whaddaya' want *me* to *do* about it???"

Here's the biggest cat and another pretty big cat and a smaller third tagging along---all three up in the kapok---but with at least as much purpose as the bigger other two. Who are we to know or not either way?

It's so much easier to think straight after dumping.

Now: they'd just swum across an inlet, or an outlet, depending on which way the water flowed. Where was the bay?

Now: they were clean. The ordeal was over, come and go as quick or quicker than a tornado, but really not nearly as dangerous.

The pigeons flew that way, away from them.

Benja looked out over the vastness. He had no home. He had his story, like they all did.

"Whom am I following?" he asked.

"No one," said Panther. "I'm just drying off. Might jump back in. Still feel dirty.

"We didn't get hit."

"It's the atmosphere---yucky."

"It was everywhere, wasn't it?"

"Seems so."

"So gross," said Kittay.

"No doubt," said Panther.

"Kind of like that limb stuff, you know?" said the Bengal.

"Their presence makes everyone feel dirty, whether or not when the shit flies you're in for a direct hit."

"I'll hook a brother up," said Kittay to Benja.

"What's that?" said the Bengal.

"She'll take care of you," said the jaguar.

"I don't want to interfere."

"Shut up, dude."

"O.K."

Kittay was an amazing cat. She'd been following the huge lost and lonely Bengal for hours before the frightened beast leapt out at Panther. She knew the cry of a lost cub, however big and adult now, still a cub always deep inside. She'd scampered and crept, leapt, crouched and kept even with the biggest cat's movements, mimicking his hesitant steps through the jungle.

Now, she knew she'd done the right thing; although she'd known nothing about the bigger cats' connected pasts.

Creepy.

Panther? Benja?

No, but so many of their stories were ... *creepy*.

"Well, I'll leave you two to get reacquainted."

"M'lady?" said Benja.

"Yes?"

"Thank you---"

"Kittay?" said Panther.

"---Yes?"

"Thank you," said the jaguar and Bengal.

"You're both welcome." She smiled and leapt away.

Panther turned left, away from the softer terrain influenced by the bay and its tributaries back there, and Benja followed. Because the Bengal was so big, he made the jaguar appear much smaller in comparison. There was only a difference of about 600 pounds or so.

There was the clearing, the latest continuing location for those rotting-fruit gorges, the Pantherville Happy Hours.

Another Pantherville. It would be for Benja, like it was for Panther. The Bengal had earned it, a safe haven, just like the rest with their stories of survival; no doubt his story was just as powerful and unique.

"Where do you want me?" said the Bengal.

"What do you mean?"

"Do I get a limb?"

"No. Yes. Whatever. Look ... Big guy?"

Benja appeared confused, tied up, stuck to the pine-needled and oak-leafed and other- debris-laden terrain. He just sat there, all 800-plus pounds of him.

"I think I need to pee. But, I can't."

"I know that feeling ... Big guy?" He put a paw on the huge tiger's neck and patted once.

"Yeah?" and the Bengal glanced over. He'd been staring ahead, eyes glazed.

"This is mine. This is yours. One rule: Hunt around and in the swamp; eat over there, too."

"That's more than one rule."

"You're right," said Panther. "Payin' attention. Good stuff." *Pat pat pat.* "You've got many new friends here. We live in unison. Somehow. Some way. Thank goodness for Happy Hour. Every day. Thank goodness I'm so mean and nasty." *Pat pat pat pat.*

"You don't like talking, do you?"

"Not really."

"Good. Me, neither."

"See ya', big guy," and Panther leapt away.

Benja peed. TMI. Not to him. He finished and kicked at the dirt thoroughly to cover the smell (cats) and slowly meandered nearer the clearing from the rough-hewn path he and Panther had been on. *That dude,* he thought, *knows where he is at all times.* Benja might, too, and soon.

He circumnavigated the clearing and smelt rotting apples---his favorite! He lifted his nose higher and picked up odors from the swamp way over there, about a mile away, maybe less. No biggie. He licked his wet nose and detected several of his favorite foods. Benja loved fresh- and salt-water fish, the bigger the better. There was only one small and salty fish he consumed, but he ate many at a time to satiate his hunger: piranha. Tigers, like jaguars, are phenomenal swimmers. Panther would've been the first to admit, though, that he'd never met another jungle cat with a taste for ... piranha?!

Benja sat in the clearing. He cried. (Yeah, all beasts cry.) Then, he saw eyes. They were late morning eyes, not very dangerous, not much fear if any, but very curious and some still sleepy-looking. He wondered if they were, indeed, friendly. He was in no mood for anything else. He was too *tired* for anything else and, despite what Panther had said about these lost souls, Benja bristled and let out a soft growl. It could've been a loud gurgle. It sounded ominous, regardless. Only the tiger knew for sure.

They'd never seen anything like Benja. They'd heard Panther growl and grouse, groan and get frustrated. But, this was different, raw, below raw, in the bone marrow, chilling and deep. There was a lot of distance and travel to the voice, the growl, maybe a gurgle. There was no doubt in the collective mindset here that this huge beastie was hurting bad, terrible, lousy, very lonely, feeling like caca, and that he needed a hug.

O.K. Anyone?

Benja was as big as a grizzly bear. He was 10 feet long, from his whiskers to the tip of his striped tail. He was one big son of a gun. He was also a frightened (if big) son of a gun. Here were all these eyes, staring out at him as he cowered like a much smaller and domesticated kitty cat in the clearing.

I am a kitty cat. There were so many eyes. He couldn't count that high. Panther said they were all friendlies---*Prove it*!

William came lumbering out from beneath a pine tree; a quiet lumber, more like a quiet twig. Realized: William is a pygmy tarsier, but still a primate, the smallest, but still has those long arms to hang from and pick fruit with and wipe his face and ass and, well, he came out from under the pine loping along on his knuckles, like a gorilla. He twigged along. William, you are one tiny monkey, dude.

Benja saw this dot creeping along. The dot walked on his knuckles, looming low, big eyes, *huge* eyes, most of his body it seemed, long ears, lumbering---twigging---along. The tiger shook his head. The dot got bigger as it closed the distance, but it would never be bigger than one of the tiger's paws.

Maybe it's dust in my eyes.

No. It's the world's smallest primate.

"Why is he walking on his knuckles?" said Chipmunk.

"Make himself look bigger," said Seysew. (Why is *she* hiding?)

The rest of the Happy Hour beasties, including newbies Amsterdam and Naja---Chimp (who knew all about the knuckles), Rachel, Elaine, Brian, Nathaniel, Robert, Roberts, Butts and Jamie, Cindy, and Emily, who could've cared less about primates and their loping and fisted strides, but she might've had a crush on Benja---crept and slithered and took off and landed again (Elaine, Nathaniel, Brian) as Benja sat and hunched over, not sure what to do. He might've been crying. Again.

Out of the corner of his eye, he noticed the dot wasn't any bigger. The littlest primate had done his best impression of a gorilla. (Really, it's not up to a pygmy tarsier to appear like he's … *lumbering*.) He'd stopped within feet of Benja's front paws. He was so tiny in comparison to nature's biggest cat that he might as well have been further away to appear tinier still, because he couldn't be big enough up close.

This might be a paradox.

The world's smallest primate certainly has guts.

William was small. Benja felt smaller. The tiny beast, no bigger than the Bengal tiger's nose, was the first on the scene. He'd been the first to depart the sets of eyes sporadic throughout the leafy outskirts of the clearing. The other animals remained on the periphery. Just a bunch of chicken shits---even, Seysew.

"I could've done a better approach than that," said Chimp.

"But, you didn't approach," said Emily.

"But, if I had."

"But, you didn't."

"I see you're still here, too."

Benja grabbed a mango and bit it in half. He chewed and swallowed.

"You want some?" he said.

"They're my favorite," said William.

Benja gave a soft toss with the half mango and it landed just in front of the tarsier, blocking his view of the huge cat-beast; such a small primate. He proceeded to bite into the ripe fruit.

"So this is Happy Hour in Pantherville?"

William chewed and swallowed a bite; whereas Benja had consumed his half in a second or two, the tarsier had a much smaller mouth. His half would last a while.

"Yep."

"Tasty ... right?"

"Yep."

"The others gonna' start eating or just keep staring at me?"

"They'll dig in."

""Why'd you approach me?"

"I don't know. I'm too small for you to eat me; barely a morsel."

"Logical."

"I thought so."

"Wasn't even a thought, eating you. Besides, Panther and I already went over the ground rules."

"I figured that, too."

"Why didn't the others figure that?"

"Don't worry about them, there's shyness in this kingdom. But, be careful with this fruit. It'll smack your senses."

"I've eaten more exotic than any of this."

William took another bite, chewed and swallowed.

"Like what?"

"Just take my word for it."

"O.K. You ready to sleep? This stuff will hit you, exotic or not."

"I wouldn't mind a hollow of pine needles and tall grass."

"I can help you with that---know two perfect spots, right below where I sleep." *Hiccup*

"I'm ready," said Benja. "But, I don't want to take someone else's spot."

"Don't worry about that. She'll find another---"

"'She'?"

"---Did I say 'she'? I meant, *you*. The spot is yours. You've traveled far, and you're the first to get intoxicated tonight." *Hiccup*

"I'm not intoxicated---*hiccup*---maybe I am. Are you sure about this?"

"Oh, I'm snoozin', too. Follow me."

The others watched as William knuckle-crawled away and the Bengal tiger followed---quite the scene---carrying another very ripe mango in his jaw. Get soused, tiger.

It remained to be seen if Benja could bite, chew, and swallow an entire mango in seconds.

Seysew might've had three or four sleeping quarters. She was, at least temporarily, losing one.

William still had a third of mango as he climbed a small oak tree to his resting place.

Benja stopped on the edge of the elephant-sized hollow, all the pine needles and moss overladen for extra comfort, and the tall grass which grew all around the hollow. It was perfect.

He chomped, chewed and swallowed the very ripe mango fruit. He looked up at the pygmy tarsier, who was still chewing on his third. The Bengal had never had such a small friend, if only because he eats so much.

"You gotta' big mouth, tiger-beast," said William as he chewed.

"I'm a tiger, not an earthworm."

"You could swallow me whole, I suppose."

"You've got big eyes for your size, little monkey."

"Night vision; they're good for that."

"I like these things."

"Mangos? Heck, I can get you a ton of those, tiger beast."

Benja sighed then burped. (*Alright, mango!*) Then, he lay down on the peat moss and pine needles, the long grass all around. That elephant made a comfortable bed. He'd have to thank him … her. That's right.

"Good night, tiger-beast."

"Good night, little monkey."

It was still light out. Dusk was an hour or so away. Sleep when you can in the jungle. The other animals were probably still at Happy Hour, getting soused on the overripe fruits in and around the clearing---after they'd extricated themselves from the leaves and twigs.

Benja would wake up later, as would William and for the same reason: Hunger. Their approach to food, their capacities, hunting and foraging techniques, were very different. Benja would go find the swamp and its surrounds, hunt there. William had merely to search in the twigs and branches around him, or pick another tree.

Now: Sleep for the smallest primate and largest cat in Pantherville; in the world, too.

Chapter 6: Ants Vs. Pigeons

"I'm only eating another bunch of berries because I can," said Chipmunk.

"Well, you should pace yourself," said Emily. "That's a lot of fruit for such a little beast."

"*Rotting* fruit," said Seysew as she used her trunk to put another overripe mango in her mouth.

"I weigh about three ounces, Em. Only William weighs less. Whaddaya' want from me?"

"So?"

"You're barely bigger than I am, cat," said Chipmunk--- "and you, tusked creature!"

"Yes?" and another mango via her trunk. *Nom nom* …

"Talk about *pacing*!"

"I didn't say anything."

"That was me," said Emily.

I know who said what---I know!"

"We're a bunch of lushes," said Seysew. "It's Happy Hour."

Emily sighed. Chipmunk grumbled.

Meanwhile … Around them and over there, further and beyond, creatures great and small continued to consume.

"Up here," said the squirrel.

"Why aren't you down here and consuming?" said Chimp, who busied himself with a whole mango, breaking pieces off. He was hungry and thirsty; alibis for alcohol.

"I've got apples back at the campus," said the squirrel. "No worries."

"Apple cider," said Chipmunk.

"More like apple jack," said Jamie, as she consumed a portion of her mango.

"'Apple rack'?"

"'Jack'."

"*Jack jack jack*!!!" said Butts, a bit emphatically.

They stared at him.

"I hear the campus tootsies talk about it."

Staring.

"Good for what ails you," as he chomped into another acorn. The squirrel pointed at Jamie. "She goes on campus, too."

Since the Bengal tiger had left the scene with William, the other beasts great and small had tentatively and furtively merged and settled into the clearing.

Wimps, thought Butts. Then: *Why am I in a tree?*

Tigers, like jaguars, climb trees.

Not the same reason.

"What's 'apple jack'?" asked Rachel, who normally didn't say much, because she didn't hang around with anyone, wasn't part of a clique, and really didn't care what apple jack was, but asked anyway, perhaps just to speak for once … in a while. She was on her second very ripe mango (she *is* a giant panda), so maybe she was loosening up with the fruity spirits, because otherwise she probably didn't give a damn.

"And what does *Jack* have to with it?" said Chipmunk, who had a bunch of raspberries and was ready to fall off the log he'd settled on, fermented fruit juice on his face and chest and dripping off the log. What a mess. What a Happy Hour. It's all about the rotting fruit and getting along---rather, getting along because of the rotting fruit.

"Get enough raspberries there, Chipmunk?" said Jamie.

"Humans call it apple jack," said Butts as he crunched away on his nut. "I heard it on campus."

Ants: travel a path of least resistance. From whence they come no one ever knows. Look down: They're there. About as welcome as pigeons; no, they're not here, yet. It was understood and a silent agreement: Ants are here, and they get into everything. They're irritating, infesting. So, get out.

Seysew looked over at Chimp who glanced up at Butts who glanced at the others in turn---"Outta' here!" said someone, maybe William. But, he was asleep.

Ants can climb trees. So can tigers and jaguars. They climb trees, are extremely dangerous and will bite your head off---but they're not infesting and irritating---and obnoxious and foul-smelling.

Yeah, everyone farts. But, there're no animals more obnoxious than pigeons and ants. (Don't forget clams.)

The red-tail hawk named Elaine landed with a soft thud on a log. Nathaniel and Brian, the crow and raven, were already on the log about a foot away.

"Watcha' got there, hawk?" said Nathaniel.

"Looks like a fish," said Brian.

"That's a piranha!" exclaimed Jamie.

"Good eating," said Nathaniel. "Tasty."

"*Eeeeuu*," said Chipmunk. He was dripping in raspberry juice, or whatever fruit he was chomping away on; could've been strawberries. No one cared to get close enough to make sure; couldn't be blueberries, because the juice wasn't bluish. Ah ha!

"You got pigeons," said Elaine. "See ya'." She flew off with her fresh kill.

"Them, too?" said Chipmunk. *Hiccup*

No one seemed to be in a hurry, after all. Happy Hour. *Belch*

The ants had stopped their march, millions of them, and their mass resembled that of the width and length of a large constrictor. Perhaps, they'd been hanging around Robert. (Mimics.) Wonder how Roberts felt about them hanging around with his best friend. There's no jealousy if you can't see them, and that a gator would be looking out for ants is improbable.

Waiting for and the anticipation of the inevitable can really suck.

Here come the pigeons.

This time, no one moved. Memories served them well: It was time for fruit (some had started early). Even the flotsam-and-jetsam pigeons knew an easy and intoxicating meal, even it was all about being social and getting soused on nature's overripe-ness.

The ants looked up, just like the others. No matter how harmless the pigeons appeared to be this time as opposed to any other, their *appearance* as always bordered on the instinctual reminder that the only thing---

"Who invited those creeps?" said Butts.

"Happy Hour isn't about an 'invite', squirrel," said Jamie. "You know this."

"Sick the ants on them," said Chimp.

"That's mean," said Emily.

"That's not a bad idea," said Seysew.

"I'd eat a few," said Cindy, a wolverine who could attack animals three or four times her size, "but they're very greasy."

"Ah, look who made it to the party," said Chipmunk.

"Been out hunting," and she glanced toward Jamie, "out by the swamp."

"How's the weather there?" said Butts.

"You're kidding."

"Kind of."

"Smart aleck."

"Yes."

"But, I did see a tiger."

"Really?"

"William was riding on his back."

"Really?"

"Where was Panther?" said Seysew.

"I don't know," said Cindy. "Am I supposed to keep track?"

"We have ants," said Chipmunk.

"What're the pigeons doing here? Don't they always crap?"

The ants remained where they were. The pigeons had landed---bounced, tripped, skid, some of them even somersaulted---and managed after their *Ouch*(!)*es* and *Ooooops*(!) and *Dammit*(!)*s* to waddle and bob and weave and--- trip some more---*Whoa*!! They stopped just in front of the ants.

There were hundreds of pigeons, but millions of ants. Communication between the pigeons was about as organized as the dodo bird's ability to fly---non-existent at the very most; at the very least, limited, disjointed, without direction, and certainly flightless.

O.K., pigeons fly, and they aren't extinct; because they aren't, no one wants to be around when they do fly.

Ant communication is all about the antennae. That is spectacular. However small the individual ant is, their power of communication is vast and wonderful and miraculous and very un-pigeon-like.

O.K., they're easy to step on.

If they're around, they can get into anything and everything.

So, they're another nuisance, like the pigeons.

All animals fart.

The rest of the Happy Hour clan stood, sat, crouched, hunched and hung in muted expectation. The ants got there first, but that never stopped the pigeons. They're not rude, they just don't know any better. Apparently, one pigeon had no idea when the other farted, but somehow hundreds could and would do so in unison. It's a miracle no one wanted.

Conversation is important in a stand-off, debate, with crime-scene objectives, classroom ethics, negotiations, compromises.

Screw that shit, these are ants and pigeons. No one gives a caca.

The other animals weren't too concerned about millions of drunken ants. The pigeons, on the other hand, didn't need any alcohol to test their already limited abilities to function in a social gathering, let alone any conversational skills when not sober; let alone it was hard to tell when they attempted take-off and flew so haphazardly whether they were drunk or sober.

"How can we hear them from here?" said Chipmunk.

"The ants?" said Seysew.

"Do we care?" said Chimp.

"Why did we back off?" said Emily.

"The other option: not warranted," said Rachel.

"If they eat any fruit," said Amsterdam, "they'll be completely out of control."

"You mean they'll shit a lot," said Chipmunk.

"How can you tell the difference when there're so many?" said Seysew.

"I'm not sure what you mean by that, but I won't pursue the thought any further," said Chipmunk.

"I know what she meant," said Butts.

"Leave it alone," said Emily.

"Ditto," said Chimp.

"You already said 'shit a lot'---What's the big deal?" said Butts.

"Honey?" said Jamie.

"'Honey'?!" exclaimed Chimp.

"Isn't she going out with a Bengal tiger now?" said Emily.

"What?!" said Jamie, who (now) apparently was going out with a Bengal tiger.

"Sometimes it's really a good thing to be so far off the ground that I cannot worry about the crap going on closer to the Earth," said Seysew.

"Profound," said Chimp, "but the pigeons fly over your head, too."

"Lotta' crap happens in the air up there," said Rachel.

Boss Ant: "Lieutenant?"

First Lieutenant: "Yes sir?"

Boss Ant: "Why are there so many of us?"

First Looey: "Breeding, sir."

Boss Ant: "No, I mean why are so many *here*? We don't need such a big contingent here, do we?"

First Looey: "Sir?"

Boss Ant: "(Sigh) We need a detour and a diversion!"

First Looey: "Can't we just tell them to move out of the way?"

Boss Ant: "They're pigeons. They might not understand."

Second Looey: "They don't even know to give a damn … probably."

Peter Pigeon, the pigeon in charge, looked over the masses of ants, a collection of creatures that seemed to have no end---just ants in a row, longer than a reticulated python, but probably not nearly as dangerous, and they most likely didn't give a damn whether they were considered that dangerous or not ... probably.

Peter Pigeon: "When's the last time we landed and the world's entire population of ants was there to greet us?"

First Lieutenant: "Never, sir."

Second Lieutenant: "Sir?"

Peter: "Yes?"

Second Looey: "I doubt this is all of them."

Peter: "All of what?"

First Looey: "Just like us, sir, there are many more of these critters."

Peter: "You would think they would've been stepped on a long time ago."

Second Looey: "Sir, we don't step on things, we shit on them."

"Do you think either group has a clue what to do?" said Chipmunk.

"Not if they eat the fruit, they won't," said Chimp.

"They have something in common with us," said Jamie.

"You really think pigeons have a clue, regardless of the fruit?" said Butts.

"Even if they eat the fruit," said Amsterdam, "eventually they'll fly again."

"Everyone farts, even earthworms," said Chipmunk.

"What about the ants?" said Emily. "Are they drunken bastards, too?"

"Ants find holes, abandoned or not," said Amsterdam. "Individually, they may get lost sometimes, but collectively, they're never stupid; quite creative and industrious. You might piss off a horde of pigeons and get away with it, or maybe get caca all over you, but never agitate a mass of ants. They're engineers---building homes, mating, collecting food---"

"And killing," said Jamie.

"Yep."

Boss Ant: "Sound off!!"

Peter Pigeon: "Sound off!!"

Ant Mass: *"We are ants!!!"*

Pigeon Horde: *"We are pigeons!!!"*

"Anyone give a crap?" said Butts. He gnawed away on a fresh acorn.

Boss Ant: "We got here first!!"

Peter Pigeon: "We got here second!!"

Ant Mass: *"We did!!!"*

Pigeon Horde: *"We didn't!!!"*

So quiet. No one had a pin. This is the jungle. No pins available. Even in their dumb-ass state-of-mind, the pigeons knew that coming in second didn't matter in the animal kingdom and punishable by death or having to kiss your sister, whichever came first or both.

"So, we got here second," said Peter. He sighed.

"We *could* just step on them," said the first looey.

"We could head for the campus," said the second looey, "and look up co-eds' skirts."

"They're not much smaller than us," said the first looey. "Maybe we could get that big old pachyderm to step on them."

"Somebody called me?" said Seysew.

"I believe that pigeon over there referred to you as 'big' and 'old'," said Chipmunk.

"I should step on them."

"The pigeons or the ants?"

"Both," said Chimp.

"Right, then you'll clean up that mess," said Butts as he chomped an acorn, "and deal with Panther's wrath and probably Benja's, too."

"The rain will clean it all up," said Emily.

"What do we do now?" said the first looey pigeon.

"Weren't we supposed to fight or something?" said the second looey pigeon---*Don't they have* names?

They're pigeons---and ants---Who *gives* a caca?

"Fight or flight, man," said Peter, who had the only name amongst so many.

Ants don't need names. They're ants.

"Fight or flight??" repeated Peter, a bit louder.

"*We don't fight, we fly*!!" yelled the pigeon horde.

"And shit," said Amsterdam.

"*We got here first*!!" yelled the ant mass. "*We are the champions---Rah*!!!"

"So bogus," said Cindy.

"Agreed," said Seysew.

"If they all fart," said Chimp, "that means Happy Hour is over."

"Not a good idea getting soused and suffocating at the same time," said Amsterdam.

"It ruins the fruit."

"Nah, there's alcohol; rotting fruit can handle it," said Emily.

"Gross."

"Agreed."

"*Eeeeuuu.*"

"Are we related?"

"Whom are you speaking with?"

"Must be the mangos."

"You kinda' look alike," said Chipmunk.

"That's not nice," said Jamie.

"No, it isn't," said Emily.

"They're both primates!" said Butts. "There *are* similarities."

"Both have such dry wits," said Emily.

"Might be the mangos," said Rachel.

"I look like you?" said Chimp.

"Who doesn't have a dry wit when drinking?" said Amsterdam.

"What's next?" said Peter.

"We can fly and shit!" said one in the horde, deep deep deep in the crowd; somewhere back there.

"Nah, wait 'til the campus to do it. We're pigeons!"

"*Fly and shit*!! *Fly and shit*!!" cried the horde.

"Nah," said Amsterdam.

"*Land and shit*!! *Land and shit*---!!"

"Go to school."

"*---Let's go to school*!!"

"Rah, rah, rah."

"Huh?" said Emily.

"What do we do?" said the boss ant.

"Well, we don't *do do*---do we?" said the first looey.

"*Took 'em to school*!! *Took 'em to school*!!" yelled the ant mass.

"I'm confused," said Cindy.

"Confident little buggers," said Jamie.

"Love 'em roasted," said Amsterdam.

"Thought you didn't eat meat?" said Rachel.

"Eh."

"I should try that---eat 'em roasted," said Chimp.

"You two are *so* gross," said Emily.

"No more gross than a cat licking herself," said Butts.

"It's what we do, you rodent!"

"Touchy."

"The jungle produces foods---flora and fauna alike---for our consumption, but not to everyone's liking," said Chimp.

"Well put," said Amsterdam.

"Change the subject," said Jamie.

"The birds are ready to fly," said Chipmunk.

"Somebody fart?" said Butts.

"Might've been me."

"*Eeeeeuuuu*," cried the ladies, Emily, Rachel, Jamie, and Seysew.

Elaine was somewhere way over their heads. Where's Cindy?

"They're going to take off," said Amsterdam.

"My farts can really stink," said Chipmunk.

"Not like mine," said Chimp.

"How do you know they're going to take off?" said Jamie.

"I can hear so many stomachs rumbling," said Amsterdam.

"Here comes a shit storm," said Chipmunk.

"The ants are gone," said Amsterdam.

"How do you know?" said Emily.

Butts looked over to the clearing from his vantage point on a branch.

"He's right," he said. "They're gone."

"How did he know?" said Seysew.

"I can hear them," said Amsterdam.

"The heightened senses of the blind," said Cindy.

"Where've you been?" said Butts.

"Hunting."

"Oh."

The pigeons flapped their wings but not all at once. Some would start to take off, and those not started couldn't get out of the way in time; a milieu, rather a melee of feathers and drool---bumping, pushing, tripping, teetering, slipping, pulling, tugging, gouging, roughing, and sloshed as they were---so many would flap their wings a foot off the ground, then the sheer weight of the crunch of a number (oh, a dozen or so at a time) of birds would grind to a flopping halt and down they'd go, bouncing off the ground. This type of group take-off happened many times, some of them bouncing off the bumping and crunching of a previous group take-off and finally some flying off if only by accident or luck or just the pigeon way of doing things, soused or not; so un-pretty to see---*really icky stuff*.

"Who's cleaning up the feathers?" said Chimp.

"At least they farted but no shit," said Amsterdam.

"Yet."

"Can pigeons talk while they fly?" said Emily.

"All birds do, don't they?" said Jamie.

"Do you walk and talk at the same time?" said Cindy.

"Do you chew your dead animal and talk at the same time?"

"Wow," said Chimp.

"Lady's talk can be deadly at times," said Amsterdam.

As loose feathers fell to the ground more and more pigeons managed to stay up in the air. How clumsy they managed to be without any assistance from each other, 'twas a built-in clumsiness and rather human of them; they hadn't had any fruit, not this time. They had no running start like an albatross always needed, no directional awareness that the other animals could detect---they seemed oblivious to hurry, comfortable with being slow and klutzy and the penultimate in procrastination. They reminded one of the dodo but able to fly when they shouldn't have been able; should be flightless birds like the ostrich and emu. It was a waste of the beauty and engineering of flight, a miracle that pigeons had the ability to fly, because they *really sucked at it*---at least, *this* group did led by Peter pigeon and his lieutenants.

"They're going to my campus," said Butts.

"*Your* campus?!" said Jamie.

"They'd better not touch my apples."

"I don't think they possess the wherewithal to fly straight," said Amsterdam, "let alone locate your hidden cache of fruit."

"How do you know they're hidden?"

"You're a squirrel."

"*We're headed for the apples*!! *We're headed for the apples*!!" yelled the pigeon horde.

"You see??" cried Butts.

"So they have good hearing," said Amsterdam. "That doesn't mean squat."

"They'll find them by accident!" said Butts. "Those guys stumble onto things---I gotta' get *over* there!!"

"They're not *here* anymore," said Jamie. "*That's* a good thing."

"Oh, yeah, sure!" said the squirrel in a mocking tone. "And if I can't bring you any apples for a while, you'll blame me!"

"Not true," said the lady raccoon with a smile. "Maybe just for a while----gotta' keep you on your toes."

The ants had resurfaced, all million or more of them; way too many to count.

"*We are the champions!!*" yelled the ant mass. Neat.

"I didn't see one punch thrown, did you?" said Chipmunk.

"Not even a spit ball," said Chimp.

"Somehow, they're the champions."

The pigeons managed to avoid most of the limbs, branches, and twigs as they headed in the general direction of nowhere. Perhaps, they really knew where they were going, but to the observers, the other animals, they looked like they were headed nowhere.

"*We're flying like champs!!*" shouted the pigeon horde.

"They think so," said Chipmunk.

"*We'll be the first at the campus---find the apples!!*"

"Now, they're going too far!!" yelled Butts.

"You know they're mimics, don't you?" said Amsterdam.

"They don't do *that* well, either," said Chimp.

"*We're the champs!!*" yelled the ant mass as they re-disappeared.

"O.K., we get it!!" yelled Chipmunk.

"Where'd they disappear so fast---*again*?" said Emily.

"They're ants," said Amsterdam. "They need the tiniest crevices."

The pigeons disappeared, thousands of them---okay, hundreds---into the jungle's wilderness, bumping away on limbs, branches, smashing through twigs and their leaves. If they could, the trees and conifers would've yelled "Ouch!" and cried "Foul!" for all the times the birds bumped, slapped, poked, careened and tumbled and whacked into and recovered, scratched and tore at and ripped along many branches, through twigs, leaves and pine needles; even the pine cones got roughed up, and they're pretty knobby and rough all by themselves.

The sap remained sticky, and every creature tries to avoid tree sap and pine tar: just too gooey and sticky. Shit (crap, caca), the daily pigeon dumps (loads, poops, drippings, number twosies) are bad enough, and stink so much worse than any tree's goo; rather get sappy and sticky than get dumped upon from above.

Butts was ready to begin his climbing of, leaping off and along the limbs and branches back to the campus; he reminded himself that the quad outside the cafeteria, along with his favorite 52-gallon plastic-lined garbage can, were susceptible to a pigeon diarrhea attack.

"I'm headed back to the campus," he said. "Hopefully, the pigeons haven't made a mess of it."

"*Eeeeuuu*," said Jamie.

"Gross," said Emily.

"Ditto," said Cindy.

The squirrel shrugged.

"I might dump along the way," he said.

"Really?" said Jamie.

"Necessary?" said Emily.

"*Ewww*," said Cindy.

Chapter 7: Komodo Gives Chase

Amongst the beasts that lurk and hunt their prey, two of the most consistent carnivores were present and accounted for on the fringes of the swamp, just a few hundred yards from the clearing; where the pigeons had managed not to make a mess of things---this time. Woe is the campus … maybe.

The two carnivores weren't alone.

It sounded like a release of air, a very long sigh; sounded of dying and the last gasp of breath but no death rattle; it was an ominous sound---sounding of death but not nearly dead---and not from around here. Now, it was. Here.

Something was in the saw grass out there, possibly nearest the swamp's bald cypress trees; the mangroves which supported so many keys big and small, some of which at high tide disappeared under the water of the Florida Bay and Gulf of Mexico. Something was out there and possibly amongst the four mangroves---red, black, white, and the buttonwood---all of which the animals needed to hide in, behind and under, above on land and immersed in the keys' murky waters, ready to hunt or escape the hunt.

Trees grew tall: the gumbo limbo, cypress, willow, oak, maple, the conifers and sycamore, and a few alien trees like the Brazilian kapok fig. There were plenty of invasive beasts, trees and plants in the Everglades and its surrounds; the trees and plants, indigenous or not, protected and gave refuge to many animals.

The carnivorous beasts headed for the swamp, where the kapok figs, willows, cypress and mangroves were dominant, where everything was damp and humid. The carnivores got busy in and around the swamp, which had its share of invasive species. The hunters, toothy beasts, knew where to get their food, but sometimes, the hunters were hunted, too.

Something …

Panther knew all about the food chain, the keystone, and how easy it was to forget---always keep a watchful eye, to protect others and protect oneself.

There were no beasts around here that could hurt a black jaguar or Bengal tiger, none they already knew about. There were few if any beasts anywhere. But, pack animals might have a chance with one wild cat, no matter how big its size.

There it was again. Or, there they were again.

Cindy, Benja, Roberts, Robert and Naja had managed to hunt and eat. Panther caught a good-sized wild boar and went up a cypress tree with it and waited for Kittay. He would share with her. They all had to eat to have energy for a potential confrontation.

Another deep sigh followed by several grunts.

"Must be Amsterdam following up with Naja," muttered Panther to himself. The other carnivores were satiated and digesting here and there.

He couldn't justify the deep sigh, like a dying beast on his last breath. Panther had a cold chill run up his back.

"You hear that?" said Benja as he lumbered up below. He had blood on his whiskers.

"Let's be on the lookout," said Panther. He saw Kittay in the distance. She must have smelled the kill. "We gotta' eat, but let's keep a watchful eye."

"Right," said Benja.

"You recognize the sound?"

"No."

"I don't, either---all the more reason."

In the swamp, there were several limbs scattered here and there, all of them "connected" or bridged by either soft mossy build-up or small boulders that had managed not to deteriorate over time to the size of pebbles or even smaller to sand particles.

Seysew and Amsterdam came rumbling and elbowing along after Kittay. They weren't following her but nobody minds a little extra protection, whether mindful of it or not. No one messed with Seysew, not even the gators or crocs, and pound for pound no one was stronger than Amsterdam. However grizzled and gray, he was still an 800-pound silverback gorilla.

Panther looked down at the turf as they approached. Kittay had climbed up and was settling in to gorge on a tusked-boar feast.

"Oh, goody," said the big cat. "You're here to protect us."

"No, we're here to eat meat," said Amsterdam. "Kidding."

"You heard it, too?"

"Heard what?" said Seysew.

"Yeah," said the gorilla. "I did. But, it ain't an 'it'."

"Goody," said Panther. "We'll have some action."

Cindy scampered alongside Amsterdam. She had blood and guts all over her face. Reminder: Wolverines are a fierce and voracious lot, and amongst the best hunters.

"Are you ever not eating?" said Amsterdam.

"I smell something really funky," she said.

"Looked in a mirror?"

"What's a 'mirror'?"

"Never mind."

"You smell rot," said Panther.

"Don't be gross," said Kittay between chews of bloody boar carcass.

"Me?!"

"Never mind," said the blind gorilla, who *saw* a lot without really seeing.

"Not jungle rot," said Seysew.

"No," confirmed Amsterdam. "This involves spoiled meat."

"*Gross*," mumbled Kittay through her bloody chew.

"Indeed." He smiled in her direction, fully aware of the juxtapositions in life.

"I know rot from my former owner in Brazil," said the big cat. (Yeah, Benja's bigger, so what?) "He used to toss the leftover feasts of pig and steer roasts into a man-made pit on the far end of his property."

"What beasts did he keep out there---er, down there?" said Amsterdam.

"'Keep'?"

"He kept you, too."

"We roamed freely, gorilla."

"Bull."

"There were no *bulls*."

"Never mind," said Seysew. She knew human slang, too. Panther might've, but perhaps he chose to forget.

Amsterdam climbed to the lowest limb on a nearby oak. He sat, and the limb shook but steadied. The other animals stared in wonder. The gorilla sat still, perfectly still. The deep sighs continued in the distance, from the direction of the swamp. There was distant thunder, the sound which echoed off trees and boulders and the stoutest and most dangerous of beasties near and far---everyone and everything felt the thunder's echo.

"There are many," said Amsterdam.

"You're kidding," said Panther.

"Nope."

"Goody."

"Would you stop saying 'goody'," said Benja. "You sound infantile."

"Nope."

"Fine."

"How many is 'many'," said Seysew.

"At least several, three or four," said Amsterdam.

"That's not many," said the African elephant.

"One is bad news, my dear."

"Oh."

"*The cat who says 'goody'*," exhaled a breathy and guttural voice, ominous, gloomy, dangerous---"*isn't from these ramparts, either.*" The voice carried like running water: creeping, sliding, seeping into the nooks and crannies of the jungle and under the hair and fur of the animals … chilling. It was over there, and other there, too. More breathing, raspy, shallow, like a last breath, not a gasp, over and over, seamless, all around … chilling.

"Identify yourself!" growled Panther, the low growl attached at the end of "yourself."

All six of them---Benja, Panther, Kittay, Cindy, Amsterdam and Seysew---followed the low and breathy voice and the shallow breathing from several or many; one is pretty dangerous.

"*What about the element of surprise?*" hissed and breathed a voice, the same one or not and none of the six of them cared. Well, eight, actually. But, Panther and Benja probably weren't counting on Emily and Chimp. No offense, guys.

"There's one about 20 feet from us---over there," and Amsterdam pointed in a southwest direction, which means squat in the jungle. The direction isn't important as far as threats go, it's whether or not the threat is hungry or looking to challenge territory.

"You gonna' tell me what they are?" said Panther.

"Maybe they'll just go away," said Seysew.

"No, they're not," said Cindy, who had a keen sense of smell, the great hunter that she was. "Their odor has changed. They're not going anywhere but here."

"Maybe if we give them fruit," said Chimp.

"Get 'em soused," said Emily.

"So, if we go back?" asked Panther of Amsterdam.

"They'll probably stay here, for now," said the gorilla.

"There are six of us," said Benja. "I'm sure they're not fools."

"Where're Roberts and Robert?" said Seysew.

"Probably still gorging out there, somewhere," said Panther, and he pointed toward the swamp.

"Naja should be alerted, too," said Amsterdam who, like Panther, was already considering the ramification of encroachment from alien sources---unwelcome, dangerous and belligerent beasties in Pantherville.

"*We have similar pasts, Panther,*" said a deep sigh, sounding near death, a wheeze.

"**Identify yourself!!!**" growled Panther.

Silence.

"Are we done here?" said Seysew. "I've got leaves and berries to eat."

"You've quite the appetite," said Amsterdam.

"I'm a lot bigger than you."

"Yes."

Shadows flicked through the swamp, wavering in the available sunlight that fought through the willows and cypresses, trees and plants with wide leaves, rotting trees, some leaning against others, blocking more sunlight, interruptions that could last years and years; then moving objects blocking more of the sun's rays, however brief the block, for seconds at a time, sometimes quicker than that, the block. A constant wheeze erupted soon after the latest brief block, a quick silhouette or a defined shadow, not sure. Rotting logs were stepped over, sometimes stopping on top, the quick silhouette with the setting sun, the backdrop light, in charge every day, but as long as there were no clouds. Shadows continued to shift throughout the swamp, other beasts, others not wheezing but perhaps not nearly so ominous, frightening and dangerous.

It was time to go, retreat for now and warn the others. Panther roared and took off and Benja did the same, their big-cat cries direct and bone-chilling, forewarning any potential stranger-enemy to Pantherville, let alone the wheezing kind.

Don't mess with Panther!

Don't mess with Benja!

And whatever *they* are, the wheezing ones ... mess with them later.

Scattering paws and sharp claws, and jaws with fangs and shark-like teeth and strength in numbers and several of the beasts leapt from submerged but still floating limbs. How deep the swamp no one knows. They're poisonous, this antagonistic pod of creatures, and they trampled through the brush and over the smaller boulders while avoiding the biggest, and the hardscrabble trimmed and bordered the swamp in and all around. The swamp: Dangerous, just like the jungle.

These beasts, they didn't roar, but they didn't need to. They were living dinosaurs, unchanged in millions of years. They trampled through the underbrush, tree limbs and conifer needles witnessing these creatures, never seen in these parts. So many of these animals, removed and plunked down via all sorts of methods---escapees of broken down labs no longer in use, exotics flushed down toilets, fallen from the hurricane skies and lucky to be alive; left to die at the side of the road after being thrown from a moving vehicle, inside a tied plastic bag, pets---no longer interesting or costing too much to feed.

"Why are we running again?" said Amsterdam as they huffed and puffed just several hundred feet---a football field's escape-length---ahead of the intruders' invasive and aggressive tactics.

Panther had an *evasive* tactic.

"We're running because we don't know our opponent whereas they probably know who we are, and---"

"Know who *you* are," said Seysew.

"---Yes, and they may have already been surveilling our neck of the woods."

"Watching us in the clearing, too," said Cindy.

"Perhaps we should invite them to Happy Hour," said Benja.

"Perhaps you should *eat* them," said Seysew.

"If I knew what I was eating."

"Just eat them---ask what they are, later."

"Funny."

"Meanwhile, you can stomp on them," said Cindy.

Later that afternoon, as many of the animals settled in for their fermented Vitamin-C, several were assigned as sentries, including Panther, Seysew, and Amsterdam.

Whatever was out there, Panther knew, had no intention of staying away. The blind gorilla seemed to know about these invaders, and that an attack was imminent. The big cat did not question him about these things. He knew all about instincts, and sometimes the less he knew or prepared for, the better. He was sure he'd figure out things quickly enough when the approach was made by whatever the mysterious and potentially hazardous visitors were about. They knew him. Panther.

The denizens of the swamp blended well in their habitat, just like the creatures that did and didn't hunt them from the jungle. The swamp creatures that preferred the surrounding and always wet saw grass and mossy terrain that bordered and merged with the boggier turf and sinkholes and quicksand--- they were as likely to wait out strangers, let them move first, get up and out and move along. After all, and no matter how dangerous and aggressively carnivorous the creatures (like a Cindy), they'd rather avoid the already entrenched creatures, however indigenous or misplaced themselves.

Panther and the other carnivores hunted in and around the swamp, but there was a mutual admiration society; indeed, some of the swamp denizens were hunters, themselves. Strangers, such as those now present, threatening and yet unidentified, weren't welcome in either locale.

Survival makes you meaner and more watchful than you ever thought capable. Even Chipmunk or a William the pygmy tarsier knew what adrenaline was.

It got really quiet. William had his paws gripped around a twig that connected to a branch that hung from a limb that grew out from a kapok fig that had been growing out of the mossy terrain since a landfall hurricane so many years ago had brought the kapok seed and so many other others from elsewhere, the Caribbean or South America. Whenever there weren't hurricanes there were a lot fewer invasive species. However far back hurricanes have land-fallen here is how far back the invasion goes---*long* time.

Silence … Then, William belched, probably from fear. Panther was on the limb that connected with this kapok. Like the tarsier, his eyes were wide open. Benja crouched on another limb directly across from the black jaguar. Occasionally, both big cats glanced up toward the tarsier: He had the best eyes.

If a cricket or praying mantis had farted, it would've been heard; audible further away than usual---at least five inches or five feet, but hurry, fart, because the cricket might be the mantis' next meal. The stink, an evasion tactic, only works for a bit.

If crickets fart on command, that's cool.

Crunch.

Snap.

Panther jerked his head. So did Benja, Seysew, Amsterdam, Cindy, and the rest of Pantherville.

The jungle went back to silence. Seysew's trunk was still wrapped around a leafy branch where it remained frozen in mid-feeding. Amsterdam leaned against the trunk of the tree that Panther had decided to climb up for his current limb; nearby, Benja on his limb; higher up, the world's smallest primate staring into the distance. The blind gorilla looked up to the other trees' branches and limbs, "seeing" with his ears and nostrils. He couldn't *see* the branches or the limbs, but he knew they were there.

A trio of silhouettes landed with a triple thud---*Phoomp! Phoomph! Phoomp!*---and loomed quietly on that kapok tree over next to the spruce; just a 100 feet separated Panther and Benja on their limbs from a trio of potential nasties. Cindy, Amsterdam and Seysew replanted their feet to face the three silhouettes, while the gorilla added a small grunt to the *Thump*!s on his chest with each hairy fist. Pound for pound, no one in this or any other beastie land was stronger than a silverback---blind or no.

No one wanted to piss off Amsterdam. The kapok tree shadows probably didn't care, or didn't know any better; if they did, they wouldn't've been looming.

Shallow breathing came from behind those raspberry bushes over there.

Just don't mess with my blueberries, thought Panther. He liked his blueberries. An acquired taste for this big cat, yes. He'd tried mangos, but didn't like them as much. He left those to William, Seysew, Benja and others. He like his blueberries, blackberries, boysenberries … *sigh* … not now.

Shallow breathing came from other there, too, near the mango tree. Maybe the critters had moved or shifted.

"**Show yourselves!!!**" roared Benja. Panther stared at the silhouettes on the limb. Neither big cat made another sound, not a whisker twitched. Benja sat in a crouch on the ground, having climbed down from the limb. The first shadows occurred with dusk, dappling and engaging his broad furry back and limbs, dancing with the slight movement caused by an omniscient if light breeze, but a consistent and subtle blow nonetheless, and perhaps the shadows from the invading creatures also danced off Benja's flanks; his whiskers, too, were shifting now with the slightest breeze. He could've cared less about the dancing shadows or the slight breeze.

He did care about his new friends. So did Amsterdam. The Bengal tiger, in his crouch, waited patiently, his tail very still, same as Panther's, while the silverback reached for a branch growing from a limb; the branch was twisted, snapped off and grasped in the gorilla's left hand; ready to swing.

Cindy leapt onto Seysew's huge back and found several fellow denizens of Pantherville up near the elephant's ears, behind them, crouching, scared---Why not?

"I think I peed on Seysew's neck," said Chipmunk in a coarse whisper.

"You did," said the elephant and "*Shhhhh* …"

From behind an elephant ear, Butts held William close to him. The pygmy tarsier was shaking.

"I'll protect you," whispered Cindy.

"Who will protect *you*?" hoarse-whispered William.

Cindy had every intention of leaping on the back of whatever and whichever beast attacked first. The wolverine was a voracious and steadfast hunter with quick and sharp claws and a strong jaw with very sharp teeth. She was afraid of no one.

The silhouettes shifted ever so slightly on the limb of the other kapok.

They're not stupid, Panther thought. He crept along his limb of choice this evening, from the same kapok he and Benja had shared just moments ago. The tiger below, sensing the other jungle cat's movement, did the same on the floor of the jungle, creeping along, slung low to the turf.

Any subtle movement by the shadows on the limb over there was mimicked by the cats on the limb and ground over here. Status quo. Any sudden movement might wreak havoc.

Bloodshed.   Panther, Benja, Cindy, Amsterdam and Seysew knew their way through the harsh ethics of a jungle.

Where were Roberts and Robert? Taking care of business in the swamp? Kittay? There might already be bloodshed out in the wetlands amongst the willows and mangroves. Panther and the others only hoped for the best, but meanwhile they had to take care of their own business, which could start at any time.

The three wraiths leapt from the limb and were in mid-air as Panther, Benja, Seysew, Amsterdam and Cindy reacted.

Roberts and Robert were joined by Naja, Rachel and Chimp, who, having been cooped up in a lab for a long time had some bottled-up anger he needed to release.

What makes a panda angry? Not enough bamboo shoots to feed on?

Protecting one's home will make anyone angry.

Creatures attacked from three sides---swamp, path, and trees---as Roberts' tail swatted whatever came in range, aiming the swatted creature toward Robert, who put a chokehold on the intruder and, though they were almost as big as his good buddy Roberts the alligator, managed to twist and roll the stunned beastie toward Chimp and Rachel, who banged on the intruder's noggin with leafy branches guaranteeing a big bump and a really nasty headache; sending the animal scurrying off and back into the swamp.

They performed this assembly line of pain many times---there were many ugly critters---and they *were* ugly.   The pigeons were a nuisance, tremendous pains in the tush, smelly, but they weren't ugly---not like this.

Damn, they stunk, too---*worse* than the pigeons. These dudes ate rotting flesh, maggots included. If they bit you, it could be lethal, much like Naja the spitting cobra's bite.

"Who are these guys?!" hissed Panther as he leapt on another intruder's back and scratched and clawed and mauled, but they were pretty tough, didn't say anything, and the big cat had his share of scratches and thrashes and pokes, as well. Panther kinda' knew who they were. It was all coming back to him.

They were fighting on two fronts. They came from the path, as well, which led into the clearing. There were more than enough of the intruders.

'Komodo dragons!!" yelled Benja as he panted his way through several swats and punches he aimed at three of the dragons. This couldn't last. It was a relentless attack.

Amsterdam sat quietly as four Komodo dragons, the largest of the monitor lizard family, crept up and closed in on him.

They wouldn't go near Seysew. They would've been crushed and stomped. But, she was ready to go after *them* if she felt it necessary. Cindy had decided to protect her smaller friends, particularly William, who'd already sent another stream of yellow liquid down the African elephant's neck.

Amsterdam was a study in calm---very zen. The four Komodos, all of them at least eight feet long, crouched low, ready to pounce, several feet from their huge quarry.

Roberts, Robert, Rachel, Chimp and Naja had returned from the swamp. None appeared the worse for wear. They remained back near Seysew. All eyes were glued on Amsterdam.

Panther and Benja had a brief respite. Their attackers had backed off, but now were headed toward Amsterdam to join the other four.

"You guys have fun at the swamp?" said Panther.

"They backed off," said Roberts. "We're good."

All eyes were on the silverback.

"Amsterdam?" said Benja.

"What?"

"You have a plan?"

"Not really."

"O.K."

"How many are there now---eight?" said Rachel.

"Ten," said Cindy.

"He appears outnumbered," said William with a shiver.

"Ten to one?" said Emily. "Yeah, that's outnumbered."

"Sort of ad-libbing here," said Amsterdam, "and playing it as it goes … no worries."

"There are ... four, five ... 10 of them and one of you."

"No worries."

Panther and Benja chuckled. They kinda' felt sorry for the lizards ... not really.

It was remarkable: Any animal in the kingdom, representative of Pantherville and the jungle at large, could stop and stare at what was going on with the world's biggest primate and his attending antagonists, and what was now in stasis, perhaps limbo, kinetic, stalled (no, not really), reconsidering (yeah, maybe, on the lizards' collective part), and so full of drama. An infrared would show several hot zones, dark red, the huge ape and 10 very big lizards.

Panther and Benja and many of the others knew this: Amsterdam---so calm. He *was* zen.

Panther breathed deeply, sporting several scratches from the claws of the lizards but no bites. He and Benja had managed to keep the Komodos' jaws and teeth away from them, however deft a proposition, and however poisonous and potentially deadly.

Brazil ... *That huge backyard*, Panther thought. That's where he'd seen these jackasses. They'd been in huge cages, which had nothing to do with him. He wasn't responsible and couldn't talk with the humans anyway. What animal could or wanted to? Perhaps, Chimp and Amsterdam; not much they'd liked about humans, anyway.

The cages had nothing to do with Panther---nothing at all. But, he'd always felt he wanted nothing to do with them, or their cages. They should've been left in the wilds of Indonesia where they belonged. Then again, so should all the creatures of Pantherville.

One of the Komodos spoke in that death-hiss, a dying sigh of sound; eerie and gruesome. He'd been staring at the jaguar for some time, now.

"You remember now, Panther?" said a hissing voice. The big cat really couldn't tell which one. It didn't matter. They were all jackasses.

"Not really." He did. Remember.

The others stared at the Komodos crouching before Amsterdam. A few were around Panther, but they already knew his reputation and weren't about to attack. Now, other

Komodos---ten of them---were about to go after a beast four times the size of the big cat.

The silverback's fists were bunched against his hips. Apparently, it was his turn to kick some ass. Benja chuckled again, which sounded like the airbrakes of a huge 18-wheeler, stuttering along a highway, attending to a newfound traffic jam.

"Oh, you *do*---remember." *Hiss hiss hiss.*

"So, what if I do?" *Gurgle gurgle.*

"We're here to redeem."

"We'll agree to disagree."

"What?!"

"You've come to the wrong place at the wrong time. I've moved on. You need to, as well. You're done here. Move along!!"

"I don't think so!!" as a low-flung sigh was followed by a death rattle (maybe it should clear its friggin' throat), which had nothing to do with dying, unless their victim was, which was usually the result, but that's not for now. Nope.

Watch out!!!

All 10 Komodos leapt as one.

Panther and Benja really didn't think they were that coordinated, but oh well.

Oh well, thought Amsterdam. He jumped up and high, reaching for the lowest limb about seven feet up, grasping, gripping, distracting all the lizards below, then roaring loud like 10 silverbacks at once as he dropped down, his legs spread, kicking out … **Thump! Thump! Thump! Thump! Thump! Thump! Thump!** … **Thump!** … and adept hands and feet clutching and grabbing air, very soon to lunge, clutch, squeeze … thrust and toss---

Four of them whimpered

(Lizards whimper … hm …)

---Four of them squeezed together in the silverback's vise-grip, the other six (or seven or eight) kicked and skittered past and slammed into the trunk of the kapok tree or swept past it, landing on their bellies behind (or in front … either side might be the front … never mind) the tree, somersaulting into raspberry and blackberry bushes, whether they liked those fruits or not.

Four lizards were clumped together in the arms and paws of a now-enraged 800-pound primate as they struggled in such a grip---How strong *was* this dude?!)---and Amsterdam swung the clump of four back and forth and back and let go with a huge **Grunt!!!!** as the lizard quartet flew through the air and landed beyond the blackberry-, blueberry-, and raspberry-entwined others, those other four that did not crash into the trunk of the tree but landed beyond, and the four whimpering and hapless dudes, each of them over seven feet long and weighing in about 150 pounds, landed on the soft turf of the jungle, not in the bushes---so lucky they hadn't landed on the roots of a willow, pine, or oak, either---*that* would've really hurt.

They lifted off the turf and slowly limped away, back toward the swamp.

Raspberry, blackberry and blueberry bushes showed marks of disturbance from a recent landing of four other dragons. Those four beasties had vanished, too. The bushes would recover.

The four that had bump heads with the kapok trunk remained behind, still a bit dazed. They, too, would recover, a learning experience.

Amsterdam had returned to calm and reclaimed his seat at the base of the kapok, back in Zen. Maybe, he was always there.

Panther and the others watched as the remaining four Komodos crawled off and headed back toward the swamp, where Roberts, Robert, Naja, Rachel and Chimp might intercept them. This wasn't Panther's problem. He wasn't the invading species here. He had been, at one time. He'd shown a bit more respect for his situation.

Kittay leapt off a limb from the other side of the kapok and ran up to the oak and alongside Benja.

"Where've you been?" said Panther from above on a limb, his limb, another one.

"Watching ... and hunting."

"Which one, first?"

"Hunting."

"How long have you been watching?"

"Since Amsterdam defied gravity and sent the ornery ones packing ... scrambling, limping."

"Yeah, you're right, we didn't need you."

"I wouldn't want to have to prove that again," said Amsterdam.

"Not me, either," said Chimp as he lumbered up on his knuckles.

"So, anyway," said the big cat (the smaller one … Panther). "What'd you catch?"

"It's over there," said a frowning Kittay, who really didn't feel the need to be chastised.
"I caught something for Benja, too, and Cindy."

"I don't need any help," said the wolverine. "I can fight off intruders and catch my own meal."

"Enough!" said Panther.

"Really," said Benja.

"You didn't fight," Seysew said to Cindy, "you were on my back the whole time."

"I was protecting William, Chipmunk, and Butts," said the wolverine.

"Yeah, she didn't eat me," said William, "so I guess she was protecting me."

"Why would I eat you?!"

"**Enough!!!**" yelled Panther.

"Bring the Komodos back … quieter," said Benja.

"*That can be arranged*," said a hollow voice with no death-rattle mimic this time; maybe, next time; 'til they meet again.

Panther roared as did Benja, again and again; finally, after several minutes, a deathly silence.

"Peace," said Amsterdam.

"I guess they might think twice about coming back," said Butts as he chomped an acorn.

"They'll be back."

Chapter 8: Butts Stroke Co-Eds

Students sat on the grass of the campus quad with a blanket beneath, a few holding hands, most staring and tapping at portable communication devices---phones, pads, laptops; others sat alone up against tree trunks and studied or listened to music on headphones or did both at the same time, headphones of different colors and manufacturers, sizes. All except for the animals had communication devices.

Those who walked as couples moved very slowly, staring at their phones, not holding hands. Some managed to converse while they held their phones. Hand-holding: gone.

Just about any conversation going on was stilted at best or at least involved what they were reading or watching on their smartphones and computers, whether they were walking along or sitting there in said stilted conversation; mostly staring at their devices.

It was summer session and no one was in a hurry. Even the professors wore flip flops. Not all. There're a few over there and they're wearing Sperry's or Merrell or athletic trainers or running shoes---but no one's in a hurry. It's hot.

Butts the squirrel sat atop a 52-gallon plastic-lined garbage can outside and across from the entrance to the campus cafeteria. His tiny and clawed paws gripped the plastic lining and Tupperware-type plastic rim beneath. From a distance, it appeared that the squirrel was a small furry gargoyle perched atop the rim of the huge plastic-lined disposal unit. Most, if not all gargoyles are ugly and scary-looking; perhaps comparing the furry rodent to a gargoyle wasn't entirely called for, not all that fair.

Panther, lurking in the blackberry bushes opposite the same sidewalk, tried to keep his laughter inward at this comparison he'd come up with----but, no, his friend wasn't ugly like a gargoyle. Not fair. Next …

Butts had an opened snickers bar in his paws. He had a knack for finding the leftover goodies in the garbage can. Panther did not deem it worthy or practical that his 250-pound body attempt the same approach---he just didn't want to get dirty; cats like clean; let alone the germ-warfare potential (cats don't like germs … Who does?). His buddy had a knack for diving in garbage cans and finding the goodies. The big cat would leave that "expertise" to the squirrel. Besides, he was exhausted from fighting the Komodos---heh, they won't fit in the damn garbage can, either.

"What is it about you that makes it appropriate that you of all animals deserve to be perched on this garbage can?"

Oh no ...

Butts chewed on the snickers, worrying at another nut, while Peter the pigeon stood stock-still down below on the sidewalk, staring up at him.

"You wanna' perch yourself up here, don't let me stop you," said the squirrel. He crunched the next peanut chunk from the candy bar, wholly in his element.

"Take you from your glory?" said Peter. "I don't think so."

"You'd fall in," said the squirrel. "You're a clumsy beastie."

"You gonna' eat that all by yourself?"

"I've every intention."

"Glutton."

"Where's the pigeon horde at? You're never alone."

"Bread crumbs. They're eating over by the pond."

"There's no pond here."

"I think it's part of the swamp, on the other side of the cafeteria."

"Who are they?" Butts pointed with his snickers-less paw, the right one, which was gooey, anyway, to the two pigeons a few feet behind the boss pigeon.

"My lieutenants."

Whatever. "You're lucky the gators and other carnivores treat you like junk food---yucky and too much fat."

"Speak for yourself, gerbil."

"Squirrel."

"Precisely."

Panther felt a shadow approach. He knew you can't actually feel a shadow, but Benja was so big vibrations from his paws' impact on the ground arrived long before he was actually … anywhere. He wasn't as big as Seysew, on, but as one of the world's biggest carnivores (a lot bigger than Panther), he was more than big enough. Panther turned as the Bengal approached, engulfed in the huge tiger's shadow.

"You don't need to be here," said Panther.

"I was lonely."

"You're too big. They will see you."

"Nah. They'll just think I'm some co-ed's stuffed animal."

"One big-ass stuffed animal."

"I can remain perfectly still."

"I should hope so."

The shadow was big and wide, the bird was flying low, 20 feet above the campus quad.

Panther looked up and sighed.

Benja became a gargoyle, of sorts, but certainly not ugly.

By now, the huge scrum of pigeons had realized there wasn't enough bread crumbs to go around; students and faculty were used to feeding a much smaller set of geese, not an out-of-hand and out-of-sorts gigantic mass of flying vermin. They had returned to the campus quad, somehow. Earthworms might be smarter, at least at handling directions.

Cockroaches.

Leeches.

Amoeba.

At least the horde wasn't poopin'. Not now … Maybe later---please, later and somewhere else and secluded.

Butts nearly choked on a peanut chunk he'd extracted from the nougat---*damn pigeons*! Shadows loomed, so many, too many, hundreds.

The snickers wrapper glowed or sparkled---both, really; then, another shadow and bigger. He let out a yelp, thrust out his paws and flung the candy bar in its open wrapper, falling back into the garbage can. Peter caught the snickers bar and choked as he realized you can't eat the wrapper, too---you gotta' extract, dude.

The bird's shadow overshot the 52-gallon plastic-lined receptacle and circled back around. On the ground, so many pigeons surrounded Peter. Why? They don't know. They couldn't know. They're pigeons.

Panther clamped his right paw over his eyes.

"Mosquito?" said Benja.

Co-eds, all five of them in cut-offs, came traipsing along the path, all of them with earbuds to their ears, dancing to whatever music gave the impetus to their shifting feet, snapping fingers, hip-hopping necks and shoulders, gyrating hips, while they side-stepped the multitude of pigeons including the scrum surrounding the flung and unwrapped and gnawed-on snickers bar; the shiny and sparkling wrapper that attracted the attention of the airborne and feathered wraith.

The squirrel slowly and gingerly climbed back up the innards of the waste disposal unit, and the co-eds stopped their unhurried forward progress because they somehow knew their favorite squirrel was about to make another public appearance, perhaps laden with slop from his current slip from the rim.

Panther saw it all unfold. This wasn't nearly as adventurous as the encounter with the Komodos, but nevertheless there were co-eds here and they represented a whole different problem, however less the violence, but certainly the unpredictability, another fiasco potentially unfolding.

Elaine eyed the shiny wrapper that bounced with leftover snickers attached amongst the scrum of pigeons. Peter tried to maintain order along with his two lieutenants, alas to no avail; all he wanted was the candy.

Butts clambered up the inside of the 52-gallon drum, reached the top and looked over the rim, his front paws gripping the plastic-bag-lined edge. The co-eds, alert, saw his posture, a rodent revealed with slop on his face. They commenced giggling. The squirrel caught sight of the girls, the snickers, the swooping bird, so many pigeons; looked straight ahead and wondered how a big-ass striped beastie thought he could hide in some blackberry bushes, no matter how still-life he became.

"My **snickers**!!"

The co-eds continued to giggle as Butts' readied to leap, his whiskers, nose and cheeks dripping with old pasta, lettuce, tomato, bits of salmon, croutons, and creamy ranch dressing. He sputtered and shook his head as he considered his situation.

The pigeons continued their liaison with the unruly snickers bar, which apparently had a life of its own---at least, according to the pigeons. It had fallen to the sidewalk, sat there, still edible, as the scrum of pigeons, bigger now, didn't seem to know what to do next. They continued to bob in circles and bump into one another. Pigeons do that. No alcohol necessary.

It was time to feel sorry for the half-eaten candy bar.

The girls squealed in delight as Butts leapt from the plastic-lined rim, his paws splayed outward, tail flattened, chin thrust forward, goop and lettuce and bacon bits dripping, flaking and fluttering with the slight summer breeze. He landed on top of the candy bar, the diving raptor closing in. The pigeons scattered as only those birds can, bumping into each other and everything else, the co-eds giggling and squealing and tossing their lacquered nails above their heads and hopefully in delight, their mid-riffed bellybuttons in plain sight and decorated by choice with all sorts of toys and ink---piercings, tattoos, statements, quotes---with beauty freckles shifting over tan lines, cleavage and puckering glossy lips. Girls and tattoos, bellybuttons, cleavage and freckles, mascara, lip gloss, toss in the laughter and squeals and a leaping, gooey and infuriated squirrel, with a diving raptor and too many pigeons tossed in the mix.

Panther had introduced blackberries ... *not bad* ... blueberries ... *eh* ... strawberries ... *smooooth* ... to Benja. They ate their clumps of blackberries, staring in wonder, something about those humans'---girls'---bellybuttons, then---

She dipped her shoulders and stuck out her rear ...

The same with *her* ...

Her, too ...

Two more, too much ...

---Both cats choked on their clumps of blackberries as five co-eds straightened back up.

"What?!" said Panther.

"What??" said Benja.

"You said something!"

"Did not!"

"Fine."

"O.K."

Elaine the red-tail hawk's claws readied to grasp. It was shiny. She had to have it. Butts had it in his grasp. He wasn't letting go. His grasp on the half-eaten candy bar indicated he was bound and determined to not let go, to find another location, perhaps more obscure, to finish his delicious and hunger-driven task, to get to the rest of the peanuts in the snickers.

The pigeons' bobbing had stopped for a moment. They might've been stunned, all of them caught up in a stupor, not the first time today, this hour, await the next stupor very soon, so soon, who knows and who cares, and perhaps they crapped so much in order to clear their thoughts of stupors. With the stunning stop, the squirrel split the scrum in two, so many to one side and so many to the other.

Panther kept chewing along with Benja, the co-eds no longer the only highlights, as his best friend scampered toward him, but not to him. Butts wasn't looking for a rescue operation, just a way out, which is a rescue of sorts; she wanted the shiny thing, she's a bird, a raptor; she cannot help the attraction for shiny things.

The lip-glossy co-eds weren't shiny, but they had boobs, belly buttons, mascara and giggled a lot. The big cats' attention spans were divided: crazy-ass raptor, crazy-ass pigeons, crazy-ass squirrel, and all that mascara and giggling. The big cats had no complaints (no crazy-ass lizards right now), but they did have blackberries, blueberries and strawberries to choose from as they watched the reality show.

The girls squealed, the pigeons about-faced for no reason, an arbitrary decision (unless they didn't appreciate squealing co-eds), and the raptor's claws extended for reach while the squirrel aimed his scamper for the blackberry bushes intending to leap over them.

Lunge.

Missed.

Crash.

Ouch.

The pigeons funneled through Butts' escape route, like a tributary grooved off a river or stream. The co-eds tittered and flung their manicured nails skyward, bellybuttons stretched, and Panther and Benja choked again. The squirrel grabbed for the hawk's tail as she passed over and snagged a quick if painful ride, extricated from the bushes, let go, landed, ouch, scampered again---*that* way, back toward the 52-gallon plastic-lined garbage can.

There was a wall, a newly-formed (hardly intended) blockade of misinformed, misaligned and misanthropic pigeons---people don't like them, they don't like people (or other animals), that's fair---who stood, immobilized with feet and brains at parade-rest; their brains were used to it.

Elaine flapped her wings in irritation, co-eds tripping over the pigeons, all five falling on their tushies; not so bad: all five had bubble-butts.

Butts considered his options: He had milliseconds. He leapt again and landed on top of several pigeons, wasn't sure if that was his intention, knocked down several, lunging, scampering, struggling, scraping, several more knocked down, dominos, the raptor grabbing for the wrapper---

Damn ...

"Is that really worth it?" said Benja.

"The co-eds on their butts?" said Panther.

"No."

"The squirrel's insistence?"

"No."

"The hawk's?"

"Yes."

---ripping some of the wrapper away, the candy remaining behind; the squirrel closed in on the garbage can, stopped short of the co-eds regaining their feet---whoopsie!---their giggling, shock with the fall, now laughing at the sight of Butts: pasta-encrusted whiskers, mouth, nose---now the salad dressing---of creamy Italian (wait … wasn't it?) and melting chocolate (milk or dark or both) and squirrel drool (*eeeeeuuuu* …) dripping to the sidewalk.

Pigeons, like fallen bowling pins were scattered here and there, splayed out on their bellies and attempting to regain their feet with no idea which way to go next.

Peter was too busy wondering how he'd lost track of the snickers, although he'd not had a grasp of the half-eaten candy bar in the first place.

Butts had scampered up to the rim once again, this time from the sidewalk, his face still in pasta-and-other slop-mode. He used his paws to wipe off the remaining residue, some of which had fallen off with his scampering, dodging, leaping, lunging, shifting, weaving, grabbing, and dropping.

Don't worry about the order of things---It's Butts, they're peanuts, they're his co-eds and the campus and its quad and sidewalks will never be the same again.

Whoopsie ... He leapt again with another fast-approaching shadow-with-wings. This time, he landed on the spaghetti-strapped shoulders of one of the co-eds, what was left of the snickers' wrapper still shining in the sunlight. The co-eds screamed, perhaps in delight, like on a roller-coaster or in a haunted house; because, they could; because, Elaine didn't hesitate to reach for the bit of shiny wrapper on the spaghetti-strapped shoulder within the grasp of a squirrel's drooling jaws, lunging as the tree-rodent tiptoed across the shoulders then over her heaving bosom, his paws jammed into her cleavage, getting stuck there (wonderful), chocolate, drool and bits and pieces of other ingredients from the bottom of the garbage can stuffed down there in the cleavage with those glorious summer freckles---screams, from all five co-eds---the raptor's wings shifting, slanting, adjusting, the squirrel's butt, tail up and twitchy, in the girl's face.

"She's not stupid, but she is persistent," said Panther.

"The co-ed?" said Benja.

"No."

"Kittay?"

"Not here."

"Pigeons?!"

"What??"

"Kidding."

"Wow."

"Red-tail?"

"You got it."

Butts leapt off and scampered across the lawn, the other co-eds attending to the one with the goo down her freckled cleavage, straps askew, the pigeons in stasis---collective if not permanent brain cramps---standing around, inert but not innate, certainly not kinetic (well, by accident) and looking like those garden gnomes but not nearly as ugly, not quite; so many beasties in stasis, brain-cramped, a stunned silence---jaguar, co-eds, pigeons, ants, raccoons, lions (none), tigers (got one) & bears (none).

Skitter skitter skitter scamper scamper ... the squirrel skedaddled back toward the big cats with the remaining snickers bar hanging tough but gooey as Elaine flew off with the rest of the wrapper---

No stasis for her or the squirrel ...

---Butts stopped just short of the bushes this time, dropped the drooled snickers, gasping for air, staring at Benja.

"Ahhh," said the squirrel *pant* *pant* *pant* *breeeathe*, "I see you've discovered blackberries."

Burrrrrrrp ... "Blueberries, too," said the Bengal.

"Stay *awaaaaay* from my snickers."

"You look terrible," said Panther.

"Thank you---*seeeee* ya'!" The acorn hunter again went back to the garbage can. Not to deal with the co-eds. Not to deal with the pigeons. Maybe to find another candy bar deep inside the treasure trove that is the 52-gallon plastic-lined garbage can.

But, first, he needed to vomit. Panther and Benja watched in muted surprise, still laying low in the bushes, as the squirrel stopped amongst the pigeons, who were again active and bobbing their heads in confusion and moving in all directions and Peter and his two lieutenants shrugged as only pigeons can, a motion that appeared to anyone else they were about to upchuck, as the co-eds stood clear of the fracas, not screaming now (please … don't), and Elaine spat out the shiny wrapper---

"Was it all worth it?" said Panther.

"Guess not," said Benja.

(They were referring to birds chasing after shiny wrappers)

---As the snickers wrapper shifted and sifted like a dead leaf toward the ground and landed in a slipshod way---*Plop!* or *Flop!*---on the same co-ed, still gooey with residue (*eeeeuuu* …) from Butts' pawing of her boobs (Alright, squirrel!!), and the king of the nuts (Butts) promptly spat up on the sidewalk.

Gross.

"**Eeeuuuuu!!**" said all four co-eds at once.

"They make a lot of noise," said Benja.

"Indeed," said Panther.

"Not much hair---"

"They shave."

"---and not much clothing."

"Back to nature."

"Ah."

Panther thought briefly about coming out of the bushes to steady his buddy while he puked, but immediately nixed the idea. He didn't want to freak the quad. There are Florida panthers, yes, but none as big as the black jaguar from Brazil. Panther: A black jaguar from Brazil.

He chuckled at the thought of Benja coming out, but then they'd know he wasn't a stuffed animal.

The pigeons took off and left feathers and crumbs in their wake, which was a vast improvement and relief over previous visits, flyovers and departures, any of the three which gave them the chance to loosen their bowels.

The co-eds leaned over the prostrate squirrel. They did not touch him. From the big cats' perspective, the co-eds' leaning-to made it self-evident that they, indeed, were clean-shaven below their necks. Perhaps, they were champion college swimmers.

Panther attempted to swallow a bunch of blackberries and choked.

"Fur ball?"

"No. Boobs."

"What?"

"Nothin'."

"Oh. Got it."

"Yeah. I was in captivity."

"They pet you?"

"No, but I stared then, too."

Butts didn't get sick from the awkward mix of food on his face. It was more from the stress in avoiding the raptor, then grabbing the raptor, then landing on the pigeons. He wasn't used to escaping with his life, although he didn't know (he forgot) that, 1) Elaine hadn't been after him but the shiny wrapper, 2) By Panther's decree carnivores could only hunt in and around the swamp and, 3) Carnivores don't eat junk food (squirrels).

Panther and Benja both looked on as the squirrel shook his tail (that noise), still prostrate on the sidewalk, his paws in spread-eagle formation, the tail-shaking normally associated with anger and warding off intruders, like humans and anyone else ready to try and steal his nuts, apples, or snickers bar containing ... more nuts.

No one was certain whether or not the squirrel laid claim to the co-eds, as well.

The girls weren't his normal interruption. (He certainly had a view no one else had, or ever have.) They leaned over their favorite squirrel and Butts kept his tail twitching, and maybe this wasn't about anger or territorial defensive measures or protecting his favorite foods.

These hairless below-the-neck and bumpy animals smelled wonderful.

Perhaps, the squirrel couldn't help but twitch, for reasons he'd never care to divulge.

"Let me know if you see KIttay approaching," said Panther.

"Why, you're not together these days---Are you?" said Benja.

"I don't know. Do you?"

"I guess I can't figure it out, either."

"Right."

"The squirrel?"

"No."

"The co-eds?"

"Next question."

"Cindy, Rachel, Seysew, and Naja?"

"Next question."

"Women?"

"Next question."

"You like blackberries?"

"That's better."

"Took me a while, didn't it?"

"Jamie," said Panther. "She'd have something to say about this."

"Wouldn't the other ladies?" said Naja.

"Next question."

"I'm tapped."

"One of them will figure it all out."

"We're not *doing* anything, Panther!"

"We're choking on berries."

"What?!"

"It's an implied thing."

"That's not fair!"

"You've had a mate, Benja?"

"Yes."

"Been a while?"

"Yes."

"Was it ever fair?"

"Um."

"You'll remember."

"I already do---Look, I'll choke on all the *damn berries* I *feel* like choking on!"

"That's the spirit."

"My rights."

"You're a male. That's your first mistake---according to them."

"Females."

"But, don't worry, they fart, too."

The co-eds grew silent as Butts raised himself off the sidewalk. He moved slowly toward the garbage can, only feet away, still queasy.

"What's your next act?"

The squirrel looked up and saw Chipmunk on the rim, gnawing on a zagnut.

"'Act'?"

"Yeah, you put on a good show, squirrel."

"Were you even *watching*?"

"Always do. Your life is exciting---getting chased by girls, hawks, pigeons, and falling headfirst into a huge can of slop. So ... What's next?"

The squirrel had leapt to the top of the disposal unit alongside the smaller rodent. Butts sighed as the co-eds looked on and smiled. His face was mostly clean of the residue, having dropped with his body-shaking vomiting. He didn't feel well, but here he was, back at the top of the can. Further away, two huge carnivores shook their huge whiskered heads and lumbered away from their bushy hiding place. No one seemed to notice.

Chapter 9: Attack Of The Komodos, Part II:

Charge of the S**t Brigade

Amsterdam, Zen gorilla, sat quietly in the shade of a willow tree. He'd become somewhat of a folk hero for his acts of bravery and strength, his heroic efforts in defense of Pantherville during the attack of the Komodo dragons, the largest lizards on Earth.

He knew they weren't defeated, gone for good. They're reptiles: even when their heads are bitten off, their bite is still lethal, fangs sharp and nobody he knew had ever killed one anyway.   You hear about these things through the jungle (grape)vines of the animal kingdom: Komodos are dragon lizards, therefore they come from Hell.

Perhaps, they should take the fight to them.

Perhaps, they'd sent enough of a message to stay away and find another part of the Everglades and its swamps and jungles to settle in.

No, thought the gorilla, *they're reptiles and their bite is worse than their bark.*

They don't bark, they hiss and breathe funny.

Worse than a kapok tree's bark, too. (Not funny.)

Panther looked up from his limb. Benja, on another, also looked up.

Pigeons.

Jamie, who was busy crunching an overripe apple and tasting fermented juice, heard a hissing sound. She looked over her right shoulder and shuddered.

Komodos.

Seysew, Cindy, and Amsterdam also turned their heads toward the hissing; heard shallow breathing.

Rachel, Roberts, Robert, and Naja were ready for another round of swamp wrestling, choking and ...

Batter up!!

(Not yet.)

The only other creature to darken the skies like the pigeons would be locusts; farmers in the mid-west know about those winged insects.

The pigeons didn't have a micro-clue (very small clue) about the situation; that their flight, incoming and overhead, had a lot to do with Pantherville shifting to the left, right, backward, forward, and "Let's get *out* of here!!"---and away from the clearing, where the tasty and fermenting fruit lay, where the hissing and shallow breathing and clawed paw-steps of the venomous antagonists seemed to be headed.

Yeah, that's where the Komodos were going.

Panther and Benja both leapt from their respective limbs and slowly stalked toward the clearing, timing their approach with the incoming movement of the giant lizards by listening for their hisses and shallow breathing, however subtle at this point to coincide with their stealthy intentions; getting louder, clearer, as they moved closer.

The animals shifted away from the center of the clearing, considering the pigeons, but upon realizing the direction of the approach of the bigger problem---giant carnivorous lizards---they thought better of their departure technique and began to resettle in the clearing. The pigeons led by Peter and his lieutenants decided it was time to land and also partake of Happy Hour. They had nary a clue that today's rotting fruit-fest had already been interrupted---rather, the interruption was a lot worse than anything they could muster, like pigeon shit, for instance.

Or, so *they* thought.

"They" were the other beasts who had reassembled in the clearing.

"They" also refers to the pigeons, who don't have much thought, not much to do with thinking, or so the others thought.

There's a cat's-cradle of thinking going on here.

The lizards probably had no idea what a pigeon was.

Nobody'd thought about that.

It might've helped that the Komodos had never been around anything quite like a massive amount of pigeons.

The pigeons: They landed in a haphazard way on branches, the ground, other animals, and each other---

"Ouch!"

"Owwww!"

"Ouch ouch ouch!"

"*Owweeeee!*"

---and they hadn't had a drink, yet.

The big cats stopped. The lizards stopped. The pigeons stopped falling, with bits of feathers everywhere.

"We're here!" said Peter, after landing on his tush.

"All present and accounted for---*sir*!" said the first lieutenant, after landing tush-wise, too.

"Some of us landed wrong, but I landed O.K.!" exclaimed the second lieutenant after landing on his feet, however much he stumbled before he came to a full stop. Unlike the others, his tush would not be sore for several days.

The other animals in the clearing had recovered from the falling pigeons. It was an irritating situation, but the arrival of the devil-lizards was a lot more alarming. Panther, Benja, and the Komodos remained as they were.

"You're one big lizard, you son of a gun!" said Peter to the lead Komodo, who just sat there on his haunches and stared in disbelief.

"What the heck *are* you?" he hissed.

"I'm Peter, king of the pigeons!"

"Not really," said Panther, "but go with it." The black jaguar was situated 20 feet away and at a right angle to the lead Komodo.

"This just doesn't look good," said Benja in a whisper, who was alongside the smaller big cat.

"First lieutenant----*report*!" commanded Peter.

"It looks like we're surrounded by big lizards, a coupla' big-ass kitty cats, it smells like fermenting fruit, there's a subtle breeze, a huge constrictor, and we'll probably get eaten---*sir*!"

"Not," said Amsterdam.

"We needed all that?!" said Peter.

"Junk food," said Panther.

"Correction, we're 'junk food', so we may not get eaten---*sir*!" cried the first looey.

"Second lieutenant---*report*!"

"I agree with the first looey---*sir*!"

"That we might get eaten and we're surrounded?"

"Yeah ... yeah ... and the rest of that mumbo-jumbo."

"I'm not sure what he said, either," said Chimp.

"*Shhhhhhhh,*" said Emily.

"Why?!"

"I don't know, but be quiet."

"We landed for the fruit, gentlemen," said Peter.

"'Gentlemen'??" said Rachel.

"*Shhhhhh,*" said Chipmunk.

"Why?!"

"I don't know," he shrugged. "I wanted to sound cool like the smallest cat here."

"That would be me," said Emily.

"Hey, *I'm* the smallest, here!" said William.

"Shut up and eat your mangos," said Butts.

"Eat *this*, acorn breath!"

"A few sacrifices might need to be made," said Peter, who seemed oblivious to any interruptions, and oblivious to the inherent and dangerous situation the pigeons were in.

"You're *birds*, and clumsy ones at that," hissed the Komodo.

"They're only clumsy when they're flying," said Butts, "because there're so many of them in the air at one time and close together."

"*Shhhhh*," said Jamie.

"Enough of the 'shushing', already!" said Seysew, who was in danger from no one. Therefore, she could *shush* the shushing all she wanted.

"Nobody wants to eat them, anyway," said Chipmunk, who happened to be on the same branch in the oak tree as the squirrel. They were both eating raspberries. About the only fruit the clearing and its trees and bushes didn't have was bananas and kiwi. But, maybe the animals hadn't looked hard enough.

"What are you guys doing here?" said Panther to the Komodo.

"What are these things?!" said the lizard, regarding the winged cacas.

"Wait 'til he sees the ants," said Butts, under his breath.

"*We're pigeons*!!!" shouted the horde of pigeons.

"We've gathered that," said Chipmunk.

"I'm the smallest here," said William.

"*Shhhhh,*" said Rachel.

"Stop it!" said Chipmunk and William.

"*All* of you had to speak out of turn?!" opined Peter to the horde.

"Let it go, sir," said the first looey.

"They're just following their leader," said the second looey.

"Where am I going?" said Peter.

"This can't turn out good," said Butts---"Don't *shush* me!!" He glanced around.

"*Shhhhhhhh*!!!" shushed the horde.

Jamie rolled her eyes. So did Panther. The Komodos stared at the pigeons. The pigeons tried to look organized ... forget it.

"I've a bad feeling about this," said Seysew, who stood on the outskirts of the clearing, while a multitude (not really, not nearly as many as the pigeons) of smaller animals sat and stood on her back---William, Chimp, Emily---just a few.

"What do we call you?" said Panther to the huge monitor.

"Kinle," said the lead lizard.

"I'm Benja," said the Bengal tiger.

"Why are *you* here?" Kinle asked of Peter.

"Why are *you* here?" Peter asked of Kinle.

"We're here to negotiate."

"You came to the right bird, Mr. Lizard."

Amsterdam laughed. Panther sighed.

"I don't think he meant you," said Jamie, who was now sitting on top of Seysew with Chimp, Emily, and William, who scratched himself. He needn't worry who could witness this act, because no one could see him anyway, even in daylight.

"I don't need to negotiate with you," said Kinle.

"Why not?" said Peter. "Because I'm a bird---You got something against birds, lizard boy??"

"*Lizard boy*!! *Lizard boy*!! *Lizard boy*!!" cried the horde.

"'Lizard boy'?!" hissed Kinle.

"Wait just a second here!" yelled Panther.

"'Boy'?" said Butts. "Wow."

"Some things I don't need to hear," said Amsterdam, "let alone see."

"Boss, maybe you shouldn't provoke him," said the first looey.

"Yeah, he's a bit bigger than you are," said the second looey.

"I could choose to chew you up and spit you out!" exclaimed Kinle.

"*Spit me out!! Spit me out!! Spit spit spit!!!*" cried the horde.

"Or, just step on him," said Chipmunk, who perched just behind Butts on the oak branch.

"Who taught them to shout like that?" said Peter.

"The troops get bored … you know?" said Chimp.

"As long as they're not crappin'," said Emily.

"Not yet," said Seysew.

"Don't get 'em angry or confused," said Butts, who crunched through an acorn. "They might do the caca thing to you."

"*Eeeeeeuuuuuuu!!*" cried the horde.

"They have good ears," said Amsterdam, who yawned.

"Yeah, but you won't eat me because I taste like *caca!*" said Peter.

"Bold. I like it."

Panther moved closer as the monitor named Kinle took several steps, anticipating an attack or departure---either way, the jaguar didn't care, he was ready.

If the lizard wants to get shat on, so be it," thought Panther.

"Boss, I think the rest would agree that we really don't need to be here," said the first looey.

"Nonsense!" said Peter. "We have numbers on our side."

"We have numbers!! *We have numbers*!!" exclaimed the horde. *"Ohh-ohhhh, say can you seeeeee, we are prowwwd of our numbers*!! *Thank you very very much*!!"

"You're full of shit, too," said Chipmunk. "But, you knew that."

"We're eating the same food?" asked Peter of no one. Both lieutenants shrugged.

Amsterdam and Benja laughed.

"What---*everywhere* I go---you're *there!*" hissed Kinle to Panther, as Benja came alongside with Cindy, Rachel, and

Seysew in his lee. She still carried a few denizens of Pantherville on her back. Amsterdam remained sitting at the base of a willow.

"If I must be," said Panther.

"Me, too," said Benja.

There were hundreds of pigeons, small and ugly; a dozen Komodos, huge and ugly; one black jaguar, even bigger and not at all ugly; one Bengal tiger, massive, gorgeous---

"Hey!"

---Handsome.

"Right."

The rest of Pantherville were to the rear, on the outskirts of the clearing. By now, the animals had left and reentered the clearing a number of times, making like amoeba.

Do not forget, William is the smallest critter here and smallest primate, as well.

"Thank you!"

You're welcome.

"Wait, you comparing me to *amoeba*??"

"Who're you yelling at, little one?" said Jamie.

"Dunno'."

Remember this: No matter who's in charge, who're the handsomest, strongest, smallest … when the pigeons are ready … Get out. No one likes to get rained on by bird doo doo, and with the pigeons' proclivity for waste dispersement by so many at once, anticipation of their departure is so important.

"We're just trying to get in on the action," said Kinle.

"Good," half-whispered Chipmunk. "You can get shat upon like the rest of us."

"What 'action' is that?" said Panther.

"You want *action*, you gotta' talk to *me*!" said Peter, pointing with his wings at himself.

"*With* me," said Jamie.

"Why am I even talking with you?" hissed Kinle. "You've got feathers! How dangerous can you be?!"

"Wait 'til they take off," said Emily.

"Flying caca-makers," said William, who remained on top of Seysew, but had moved to her head and between her floppy ears. He was safer up there from the lizards, but not from the pigeons. They never knew where they were going, which made it very tough to plan ahead before they needed to dump.

"They don't care where they drop," said Chimp, "they just care that they do … drop."

"When you gotta' go, you gotta' go," said Emily.

"We could change the subject," said Seysew.

"What *action* are you talking about?" said Benja. He had moved closer than any of them to the Komodos. When you weigh 900 pounds, you can get as close as you want. That goes for Seysew, too, who weighed a lot more than that.

Amsterdam: Always Zen.

"This is Pantherville, right?" said Kinle.

"That's right!" yelled Butts.

"We'd like to rename it Komodoville."

"You're kidding," said Cindy in a half-whisper.

"I don't think so," said Amsterdam as he lifted himself off the ground and slowly elbowed his way toward the increasingly irritating lizards. Nothing was more irritating than the flying poopers, unless the two groups were in the clearing at once. Here they were.

"*Ohhhhh*, I know what kinda' action *you* want, lizard boy!" said Peter.

"I just told you, pigeon, or whatever you are," hissed Kinle, as he kept glancing left and right, as the other lizards did; observing the encroachment of Amsterdam, Benja, Cindy, Rachel, and Seysew and, looming, Roberts, Naja, and Robert. Carnivores, all, except for Rachel.

Don't mess with a giant panda.

Panther shook his head and realized how much he didn't care what this place was called---Who'd named it Pantherville, anyway? Not him.

"You want all this fruit to yourselves!" claimed Peter.

"Do we look like fruit-eaters to you?!" hissed Kinle.

"*Fruit eaters*!!" yelled the horde.

"That was ... succinct," said Emily.

"I really don't know where they get it from," said Peter as he glanced back at the horde.

"Boss, I think it's time for us to leave," said the second looey.

"Yeah, I agree," said the first looey.

"We can stay and defend our territory," said Peter. "It's our fruit, you know!"

"What?!" said Chipmunk.

"Easy, killer," said Seysew.

"Boss, they're hissing," said the second looey. "You know?"

"They always hiss!" said Peter.

"True," said Chimp.

"Indeed," said Emily.

"Don't touch my mangos, you *bastards*!!" yelled William.

"*Your* mangos?!" said Rachel.

"He shares," said Jamie.

"Big deal, what's a 'hiss'," said Peter. "We can fart, you know!"

"Oh no," said Emily.

"Oh yes," said Chimp.

Please do---great idea! thought Butts. *Wait … what am I thinking*?

Panther smiled to himself as the pigeon horde started shaking their butts and flapping their wings.

Kinle and the other dragons had quizzical looks on their faces. They had no idea what were in for … déjà vu of a different kind. (Remember: Amsterdam.)

"It's probably best if you get out of here!" yelled Chipmunk. "All of us get out of here!"

"Boys!" yelled Peter. "It is time!"

The lizards collectively grumbled hisses … If Kinle could've, he would've scratched his head. He could not.

"Ohhhhh, we're off to see the wizard, the wonderful wizard of crap!!!" shouted hundreds of flying caca makers.

"Everyone head to the bay!" yelled Chipmunk. "It's dump time!"

"Where'd they get that one?" said the first looey.

"Probably heard it on campus," said the second looey.

"Taking off!!" yelled the doo doo bird horde.

"This can't be good," said Amsterdam.

"To the bay!" yelled Panther.

The monitors really had no idea.

Like an old garden hose after the water is turned on and the tears in the fabric are made apparent, the pigeons weren't about to control themselves---*couldn't* control themselves---as they released a white spray with their usual fumbling bumbling take-off; diarrhea squirted everywhere as so many birds tripped skipped flipped and careened into tree trunks, branches, tall grass, each other, and other animals.

The Komodos hadn't reacted as quickly as the others (How would they know?) and hadn't a clue regarding the pigeons' potential for dumping. They were hit hard, a real soaking, very stinky, and all the lizards were bombarded with the klutzy birds---they bounced into and among the uninvited guests, who became white dragons, anointed by loose birdy bowels, and they whimpered did the dragons like lost puppies as the caca blasters regained their footing to take off once again, missed, stumbled, tried again; liquid poo everywhere, a lot of it coated and dripping from the dragons.

The lizards spun in circles, rolled on the ground, slicked in white, tripped over themselves, yelped, screamed (that's a new one), gyrated, flopped, slipped, plopped, whimpered (old news), spun, even flipped and somersaulted, but everywhere they turned there was shit, more crap, so much caca, all that doo doo, messy messy in white poo poo.

The animals from Pantherville headed toward the beach as the pigeons mismanaged their way over and around and sometimes through the trees, between branches and twigs, leaving drips and drops everywhere, feathers, too; the sound of farting, the atmosphere going green with all that methane---the Komodos are bad news, the pigeons are worse---as they closed in on the bay, only yards behind the Pantherville gang, who had yet to be whitewashed, slathered in slop.

The Komodos moved as fast as giant lizards could move over the uneven terrain, not looking up to see the pigeons careening through the air and trees as they passed underneath and closed in on the bay---

Splash splash splash splashsplashsplash ... Splash!!!

Panther and the rest hit the water one after the other and sometimes at the same time and even in a group and---

Splash splash splash splash splash splash splash!!! The Komodos hit the water with relief. Get rid of that crap.

The pigeons, still airborne, streamed in over the dunes in their usual haphazard way but not crappin' anymore and swooped low over the water where all the animals except Elaine and Brian and Nathaniel pummeled the water, cleaning themselves off, but only the Komodos got hit, drenched, smothered, slathered and coated, but everyone felt dirty and gooey and icky (*eeeeuuuuuuuu* ...), even the trees and plants. Now, everyone was washed off and now the bay and its water felt really dirty ... not really. Water has no feelings.

All the animals looked skyward in earnest. The pigeons thought better of landing in the water. They weren't that stupid.

No one wanted to eat any of them anyway.

Meanwhile, there were three birds who enjoyed an occasional Happy Hour (they weren't much for fruit) and were perched on a log in the sand. They conferred on the developing drama before them.

Nathaniel: "Looks like the pigeons won this round."

Elaine: "They look very unappetizing---I'll pass."

Nathaniel: "You like shiny things."

Elaine: "Not to eat, stupid."

Nathaniel: "Our bad."

Brian: "You're picky, aren't you?"

Elaine: "I have special needs. I'm a carnivore."

Nathaniel: "Well, whoop de doo. I'm a crow. I'll eat anything, even fast food."

Brian: "Same here, but I'm a raven, so I have a *bigger* appetite."

Elaine: "You two eat junk."

Brian: "So?"

Nathaniel: "Yeah ... So?"

Elaine: "I'm outta' here!" (She flies off.)

Brian: "We won't miss you!"

Nathaniel: "Nope."

Brian: "Well, maybe we will."

Nathaniel: "Yep."

The beasts, antagonists and protagonists, heroes and villains alike, continued with their salt-water bathing; though the pigeons had flown on and up the beach, skedaddled, with no real flight pattern, as always, and went to bug the clams and crabs and seaweed and sand and whatever else they could irritate, alive or dead.

Meanwhile ... about 100 feet away and busy swimming in a circular and frenzied and organized group: Piranha.

"What's that?!" cried a wet and dripping William---all three ounces and four inches of him---as he rode the equally wet and dripping back of Seysew.

"Fish," said Jamie, as she also rode Seysew's back, wet and dripping. Indeed, the elephant sat in the water, about 10 feet deep and hosed down her friends with her trunk. "Dangerous fish."

"Sharp teeth," said Chimp, also wet and dripping on Seysew's back.

Remember, the pigeon goop never hit them. But, it's the icky (*eeuuu* ...) thought that counted.

"Good eating," said Roberts, as he flopped in the water, all 1200 pounds of him.

"Perhaps, we should send the Komodos over there and introduce them to each other," said Cindy.

"Piranha don't say much," said Panther as he and Benja swam around alongside each other, "a useless endeavor."

"See if the Komodos are hungry?" said Amsterdam. He sat on the beach, close to the water's edge. He was a Zen creature and would get in the water when he damn well felt like it.

"Why not?" said Benja. "It might be fun to watch."

"Whatever," said Panther.

Most of the animals splashed away in the bay and, although none from Pantherville had been hit by the pigeons' waste disposal, they still felt it necessary to be cleansed. They'd been close enough to the release point to feel slimy and smelly and icky just being in the general vicinity.

The Komodos climbed out of the water. Now, they were hungry; most are after swimming.

"I suppose we have the same allowances for hunting and eating? said Kinle.

Panther had let himself out of the water, as well. He stared down the beach toward the approaching mass of piranha. He looked back toward the lizards.

"Yeah, you can hunt in the swamp and around it," he said, "just like every other carnivore here. Meanwhile you wanna' snack?"

"Awwww, I was gonna' eat them!" said Roberts. He was still in the water.

"Not this time."

The Komodos looked out toward the water and saw the carnivorous fish. The rest of the animals had left the bay, except for Roberts. He loved the water. He also loved eating piranha.

Not this time.

"Snacks!!" yelled Kinle.

"All that fighting avoided for the love of food," said Panther.

"A full tummy beats bruises any day," said Benja, who realized it might get kind of crowded for the carnivores at the swamp. "You think the swamp's got enough food for Cindy and the lizards?"

"Cindy might eat the lizards. Our troubles would be over."

"She's got that much of an appetite?"

"I don't know."

Like all fish, the piranhas have eyes that don't shut; they seemed wide-eyed as the Komodos charged towards them through the shallow water.

Then: A feeding frenzy, fast and judicious similar to the piranhas' innate ability to attack and feed. Now, they were susceptible and in big trouble; these lizards surprised none of the other carnivores with their mass-utility and –ability to swarm and consume a ready meal; as ready as the piranha managed with their own meals, now a feeding frenzy with them on the menu. Nature: giveth and take away. The toothy fish had no chance. Several belches were heard from the dozen or so Komodos, who ate bones and all, chopping and chomping away; sometimes, just swallowing whole.

The vitamins, nutrients and protein are there, chopped up or not.

"You think we might scout some more of those?" said Benja.

"Why?" said Panther. "The swamp area is bogged down with food."

"You made a joke."

"I did? ... I did. Besides, there are only a few of us who like fish that much."

"It's a pain in the ass swimming for fish in the swamp."

"There might be a few things in the swamp that can eat us."

"A few of Roberts' and Robert's relatives?"

"Where ever the apostrophes may fall."

"Huh?"

"Never mind."

"The lizards seem satisfied."

"Burping means too much air with the consumption---eating too fast and talking too much."

"At least we don't talk too much when we eat."

"No, that's humans; especially at picnics. That's where the ants have their fun."

"They eat humans?"

"C'mon, Benja, you're kidding."

"I am."

Both big cats, totaling over a 1000 pounds, had a chuckle.

"What about farting?" said Benja.

"Everyone farts."

"I see bubbles."

"Yeah, lizards have gas, too."

"It's a good thing they're in the water where we can see it before we have to smell it."

"Descriptive."

"Should we warn everyone?"

"You have a thing about crapping, don't you?"

"Dumping's important shit … stuff."

"Farting carries its own warning. The others can fend for themselves."

"We could change the subject."

"We could also get out of here before the lizards leave the water."

"Or, the pigeons come back."

"Nasty."

Chapter 10: Strike That: Lightning

They left the water and slumbered on the sand. There was no one there left to confirm their departure after their fish-fest or their sleeping on the beach.

With the summer dusk, clouds billowed awake and layered quick and sporadic but with no hesitation---some ran out of moisture, some didn't depending on updrafts of humidity and methane from farts below---towering cumulonimbus giants, capped with anvil-shape tops that sheared with the ionosphere, absorbing the weaker and less-static growth; what were once six or seven stratus became two or three nimbus thunderheads.

The beasts, including squirrels, raccoons, panthers, a tiger, an elephant, and other various creatures, took to their individual hideaways and hovels, some under the leaves and needles of trees and conifers, others in burrows in the ground or old tree stumps and logs, holes in the bark oak and willow, all with the notion of letting the latest storm pass over and through.

Panther found a heavy limb down low about 10 feet off the ground in a kapok tree, a huge tree and, like him, not indigenous to Pantherville.

Benja was behind, closer to the trunk of the same tree. The limbs of a kapok could hold two huge cats like these, none of the three native to the Everglades.

Like tornados, lightning can strike anywhere anytime with the right static build-up, but it would be difficult to hit the cats on such a low limb in such a big tree with so many other limbs and other leafy trees and needled conifers providing electrical attraction and therefore tremendously lowering the odds.

Seysew found some tall grass close to the clearing and also surrounded by trees. The rains that came down and their individual droplets found ways to slip through the leaves, bouncing and sliding off, soaking so many. All leaves get hit even with the slightest of rain showers. Plants and trees aren't looking for cover, anyway.

Those formerly sitting on Seysew's back and head---Jamie, Chimp, Emily and William---were now huddled under the lush leaves of a willow tree. Others, like Amsterdam, Roberts, Robert, and Naja, simply squatted or stretched out in the rain. For the silverback, it was a bath. For the gator and snakes, they hunted in the water.

"Why are you in this hole with me?" said Butts.

"Is this your hole?" said Chipmunk.

"You guys gonna' let me in?" said William.

"No!" said the squirrel. "It stinks enough in here!"

"You smell worse than I do!" said Chipmunk.

"I thought you bathed!"

"I thought *you* bathed!"

"Damn close quarters!"

"Some of these raindrops are bigger than I am---let me in!"

"Fine, get in here!"

"What if he stinks worse than us?"

"Be thankful the pigeons aren't around. Their smell *really* permeates."

"You look like an earthworm with two eyes when you're wet," said Chipmunk to William after he'd squeezed in.

"I can't help it if I'm small, you rodent!"

"Harsh," said the squirrel. "But, apt."

"You callin' me a 'rodent', you pygmy primate?"

"Harsh, but let's shut up. These are close quarters."

"I *am* a pygmy primate, stupid!" said William.

"You fart in here," said Chipmunk to William, "I'm throwin' you out!"

"I'll kick your ass!"

"I'll kick *your* ass!"

"Shut up," said Butts.

"If I have gas, that's my problem---*not* yours!"

"*Shhhhhh*," said Butts, "Sleepy time."

"Fine, I want to hear the grass grow, too."

Lightning flashed and thunder boomed in the near distance.

"You think we'll get struck by lightning?" said Chimp to the others.

"There's always that chance," said Jamie.

"Lightning's tricky," said Emily. "It finds a way."

Rachel elbowed her way over to Amsterdam, who sat silently against a willow, contemplating existence, or bananas, or his loss of eyesight, or all three; a Zen-beast; always attainable to him.

"I smell beauty," he said, not looking right at the giant panda, as he was sightless. Rachel had approached from his left.

More thunder. Closer.

"Thank you," she said. "You're getting wet out here."

"It's good that one of my senses takes a bath while another cannot enjoy the dimmest of light. It helps me forget the loss."

"I see," she said. "Well, of course I can see---sorry."

"Don't apologize. It is nice of you to visit---and you smell good."

"Can I sit out here with you? I don't mind the rain."

"Lightning."

"I'll take my chances, too."

"As long as you don't mind if I fall asleep."

"Not at all."

"You *farted* in here??" said Chipmunk.

"I'm nervous," said William. "Thunder makes me very nervous."

"He's gonna' pee, next," said Butts.

"What are you, a *puppy dog*?" said Chipmunk.

"No, I'm a pygmy tarsier---you already *know* that!"

"Never mind---*point your ass out of the hole next time*!!"

Jamie decided she needed some privacy for her constitutional. She circumnavigated the willow tree she and the others formerly on Seysew's back and head had settled under. She stopped on the other side of the willow's trunk.

A lightning bolt---**BAM!!!**

The searing light was brighter than the sun, up close, a white flash of intense heat, the flash which lasted less than a second, but the glow and its imprint on the eyesight of every animal nearby who'd managed not to have their eyes shut lasted for many seconds afterward; as several beasts were tossed up and out, banging into branches, landing in the clearing and flipping and bouncing and skidding and all three until they stopped, upside down or flat on their backs or prostrate on their bellies. The simultaneous clap of thunder and its resounding reverb ricocheted violently off the nearest trees and limbs, boulders, the willow tree blown up and its smithereens crash-landed near and beyond with racketing cracking popping sound and one creature was laid out cold if not dead … Gone … Deceased. Jamie.

Kinle and the other dragons scampered through the storm as fast as their stumpy legs would carry them. Their new-found settlement, about a mile around the other side from the hunting territory established near and in the swamp, had rapidly flooded with the current deluge from the latest tropical squall to slam through. What started as cirrus clouds and haze back towards Mexico and Cancun Island had methodically developed and strengthened into its current cyclonic condition, wreaking havoc across the Gulf and its shipping, fishing and cruise lanes, saturating the Tortugas, Key West, Marathon, Islamorada,

Lower and Upper Matecumbe Keys; now attempting to drown flora and fauna in the Everglades and ... Pantherville.

The Monitors appreciated water like any other beast, but this was too much. Now, they were scampering west to avoid drowning.

For Panther, Jamie, Butts and the others, Pantherville was home, and whether they were let go by a bored pet-owner and dropped at the side of a road, flushed, thrown in a garbage can or dump, or escaped from or let out of a lab or zoo, or "dropped off" by a hurricane, or a "victim" of overbreeding, this hodgepodge of beasts of domesticated or wild origin were now all wild, some not by choice---that a black jaguar could get along with a campus gray squirrel was what Pantherville was all about.

The Komodos reached the edge of the rotting-fruit-laden clearing. With the downpour, the clearing's cornucopia of settled fruit was transformed into fermented slushies; no cups necessary. Drink that puddle and get soused.

"We're getting flooded out!" yelled Kinle.

"Climb a tree," said Panther.

"Lightning."

"Climb a rock."

"You're kidding."

"Find an elevated cave."

"Hmmm ... didn't think of that."

Chasing the lizards and not slowing down was a flash flood. The swamp, always at a high saturation point, was responsible for the chase. It had some help from the latest squall. Panther looked over the shoulders of the lizards and through the pouring rain at the oncoming rush of water pounding through the jungle.

"**Move!!**" he yelled.

The smallest animals climbed trees; up high they went--- Butts, Chipmunk, William, Chimp, and Cindy. The bigger animals, including Panther, Benja, Seysew, Rachel, and Amsterdam with Naja, who wrapped herself around his bulky shoulders, made a run for it. Every one of them except for Seysew could also climb, but they had the speed and size the other smaller beasties did not to escape the flash flood.

The lizards swam and grabbed ahold of loose branches and limbs and hung on. They could've done that in the first place, but maybe they felt honor-bound to warn the others first.

Doubt it.

Roberts swam alongside the lizards. He was used to the water. He might've been humming to himself.

Robert, the reticulated python, had wrapped himself around a limb higher up. He had no reason to keep ahead of the flood waters, which rushed on below.

The storm would end and the flooding, stop. The animals and the Everglades were used to such tropical squalls, however sudden their appearance. Sometimes, it just rained a lot. This time had been particularly intense and drenching. A hurricane: much worse.

Meanwhile, a drenched and coughing raccoon climbed a very wet willow tree to a limb. No one else was in the tree.

The ants were safely underground. The water wouldn't reach them. They knew how to build huge and weather-safe underground burrows with interlocking avenues going down and up and this way and that; big and complex enough for millions of ants.

Peter and the pigeons sat soaking in several oak trees. It wasn't flooding up there but they were rather wet from so many raindrops.

"We couldn't have picked a drier tree?" said Peter.

"There isn't a drier tree," said the first looey.

"No, they're all wet," said the second looey.

"*How dry I was!!*" shouted the pigeon horde, hundreds of them dispersed through several wet trees, all the pigeons soaking wet but not flooded out. That wouldn't be good. It was tough enough to deal with them let alone when they're waterlogged. Farts are bad enough without being wet.

"So many wiseasses," said Peter.

"Well, they speak the truth, sir," said the second looey.

"Indeed, they do," said the first looey.

"*The truth shall set you free!!*" Hundreds of pigeons, however wet, started singing in unison---

"You had to agree?!" said Peter to his lieutenants ... looeys.

---"'I can see clearly now the rain has gone'!!"

The first looey stared at the second looey.

"Did you teach them that?"

"They're singing on-key, too---but, no, I did not."

" ... gonna' be a briiight---!!"

"Briiiight!!"

"---Briiiiight bright bright sunshiny da-yay-yay!!"

"I'm gonna' barf," said Peter.

"That's terrible, sir," said the first looey.

"Anyone sounds better in the rain---even us."

"Gets rid of stinky poo, too---sir!" said the second looey.

"What??"

"Sometimes I land on a dormitory window sill and watch."

"What?!"

"*Slowwwww riii-hiiiiiide ... take it eezayyyyyy!!!*"

"Go ahead, sir, vomit," said the first looey.

"No, actually, I like that song."

"Where's Jamie??" growled Panther. They continued to scamper, but had slowed a bit, the flooding beginning to abate and settle.

"I don't know," said Cindy. "It wasn't my turn to watch her."

"That wasn't funny," said Amsterdam.

"It wasn't meant to be."

"She's up a tree, I believe," said Seysew.

"Seriously?" said Panther.

"I can see her from here."

"Wish I had your eyes," said Amsterdam.

"I'm sure you once did."

"No, not that good."

"I'm tall, you know."

Seysew had no problem taking her time in the current of a flash flood. This was no hurricane, whose flood waters can go on for hours, days, however long. Seysew was very big, had very strong legs, and had a trunk that could grab on to stationary objects heavier than she, like a huge kapok tree or old oak.

"She's safe?" said Benja.

"She is," said Seysew.

Panther leapt on top of the lady African elephant and tiptoed to the top of her head---

"Which way?"

"Other way."

---Stared in the opposite direction which he started staring, nodded, and climbed down.

The heavy rain had slackened to a light shower. Lightning bolts connected with the ground here and there and, since the ground was over-saturated and ponding, the bolts that lit up were accompanied by very loud, spontaneous and crackling thunder, reverb and echo on full volume, teeth- and fang-jarring vibrations included.

"We really don't want to be out here," said Rachel. "It is still rather dangerous."

"It's not like any of us own a house," said Amsterdam.

"Huh?" said Cindy.

"Never mind."

Amsterdam had been part of a research team and knew something about humans and their protective enclosures of wood, stucco, brick and mortar, steel and glass.

"Humans are more likely to be reckless about this weather than the rest of us," said Panther.

"You mean *stupid*," said Jamie.

"Synonymous with 'reckless'," said Emily.

"Agreed," said Butts, who'd come out of nowhere and knew something about campus and backyard trees and their branches and the humans' homes and businesses visible from said trees.

Panther at one time had a rich benefactor.

"Hey, big guy?"

"What's up, little guy?"

"I think Jamie's injured, struck by lightning."

"What? Nobody told me!"

"I just did, dude."

"She's fine, Panther," said Seysew.

"Well, go get her!"

"I'd let her be," said Kinle. "She's recovering."

"Who asked *you*?!"

"Nobody, but I've experience."

"Let me guess: You've been struck by lightning!"

"Well, no, but my family was."

"Your 'family'?"

"My mate and three children."

"Oh ... sorry."

"I take it they didn't make it," said Seysew.

"No."

"Well, I'm sorry," said Panther.

"We're all sorry," said Seysew, and she took off back toward the clearing and the remaining slosh to rescue Jamie from a tree.

"How long has it been?"

"Three years."

Jamie lay very still on a limb far enough above the receding flood waters. At this point, she didn't care what happened, and if another storm was imminent (there wasn't), she was way too exhausted and in pain to be concerned. Getting struck by lightning will do that.

"Hello, Jamie," said Seysew. She was just below eye-level to the raccoon's chosen limb in the kapok tree.

"Hello, Seysew. Panther screaming, yet?"

"Uh, yeah. You O.K.?"

"I think I was struck by lightning."

"That must've hurt."

"I guess I should be dead."

"You're not. Panther's insane with worry. So, your being alive will stop that. Then again, I've never been accused of being an angel. So, I guess you can't be dead."

"I don't think I understand."

"It's a human thing. Forget it."

Jamie very gingerly climbed onto Seysew's raised trunk, which she'd attached to the limb. The water had receded to its near swamp-state which, out here in Pantherville and not far from their favorite rotting-fruit-laden clearing, it was hard to tell as always where the swamp ended and the jungle began.

But, no *slurp* *chomp* *gulp* or *swallow* right now. No one wished to be a drunken fruit-lush, especially after this severe summer storm.

Back at the bay: It wasn't until the overwhelmed swamp and its flash-flooding had receded that Panther, Butts, Kinle, Amsterdam and the others realized that the bay was so close. The flooding had happened suddenly, in such a hurry (a flash-flood), and there were so many spontaneous currents and rivulets that weren't there before and would be gone soon enough. No one had even the quickest glimpse at the normal waterline of the bay: The flash-flooding rushed over the lip of the breaking waves well before and finally merging behind the stormy and breaking surf, about 50 to 60 feet into the bay. The curtain of heavy rain made it impossible to see more than 10 feet ahead, and surviving the sudden feeders from the swamp was an all-consuming, -encompassing, -engaging and, well, you gotta' survive, first and foremost.

"I don't care, lizard!" said Butts. "I saw her on the limb long before you did, ya' scaly bastard!"

"Then, why didn't you say so?" said Kinle. The other lizards were staring toward the now re-visible bay, where another round, or mass, of shifting swirling spinning (and tasty) piranha moved along the bay's edge, just behind the breaking waves, a light rain still falling and droplets dimpling the surface.

"Because, I wasn't here, yet, and then you opened your big fat mouth before I did, anyway!"

"Shut up---both of you!" said Panther.

"I'm fine," said Jamie "I'm O.K."

Kittay strode alongside while Jamie rode on top of Seysew.

"Ah," said Panther. "You made it, too. That's good."

"I tried to save the kill," said Kittay. "It was gone."

"It wasn't worth it. That wasn't smart. You're lucky."

"I know."

"Forget it. You're here. That's all that counts."

"What does it matter who saw her first, anyway," said Chipmunk, who'd followed Butts, Chimp, Emily, and William through the trees.

"Hey, I'm just hungry," said Kinle. "I don't care."

"You gotta' worm?" said Amsterdam.

"What? No, I like to eat, ape!"

"Besides, she can take care of herself," said Emily.

"Which one?" said Chimp.

"Kittay or Jamie?" said William.

"**Both!!**" growled Panther, who eyed the lizards eying the piranha and wondered, "Why couldn't they just drown!"

"They"---piranha or the lizards? Pigeons?? Ants???

"You guys oughta' just stay out here and eat fish," said Amsterdam.

"We've got fish at the swamp," said Kinle. "Why stay out here?"

"I don't know, maybe the sharks'll getcha'!"

"Jackass …"

"**Shut up!!**" roared Panther.

Amsterdam chuckled.

Benja shook his head.

Kittay helped Jamie off the elephant's trunk.

"The next time I'll ask the red-tail or the crow or raven to fly me here quicker!" yelled Butts. "The next time a flood hits and the swamp decides to overrun the bay and you friggin' lizards come chasin' after more piranhas!!

A lightning bolt seared the sky, jammed into the trees and speared the water in the bay, exploding with a wet and thunderous crack-splash, sound waves and the brightest light slammed back through the animals, bone-jarring, crashing back through the clearing and drilling the swamp with burst-echoes, pile-driving sound that wouldn't stop. The animals' aural canals took on a ringing sound, scratchy, too, an irritating level note like that of a flat-line only scratchy, like an old record, a human thing, but they couldn't hear a thing now; the echo-rumble---really loud---thunder bouncing and pounding into the distance, the bay's beach a cloud of wet sand, its minute-dust soaked and floating, bits of dust caking together, a bit more sting in the still-stormy air, a light rain still falling, the piranha no longer on the move but dead from electrocution; the lizards still flattened like the others on the wet sand; and the debris-laden mud of the path vibrated, shaken by the claps of thunder to an exhausted stillness with nature's blast of electrons, protons and neutrons; in charge, charged up, an ionic thrust and display of noise.

Ringing ears, everywhere. Scratchy sound, too, like static. That was weird.

"*Whatdidyousay*---Call me a *what*?!"

"I can't hear you---wait, *that's* not nice!!"

"You said what??---You never even met my mom!!"

"I've got a ringing sound---Hey!! Up yours, too!!"

"Wait, I can't hear---Wait a sec---*You* can't call me *that*!!"

Hundreds of pigeons watched millions of ants come streaming out of the ground, like from a metal faucet they'd seen on campus, although these ants would never depart their hideaway that way, because they built homes in the ground, not inside the wood, cement and metal.

What kind of ants were these?

"*We're the best*!!!" shout-sputtered the ants. They were pretty wet.

As the remaining water flowed from their flooded residence---

Wait …

Never mind …

---*All* the ants received the same treatment, i.e., they were each spat from the earth, landing softly on their tushies---

"Ow!!" "Ow!!" "Ow!!" "Ow!!" "Ow!!" "Ow!!" "Ow!!"

Loud little bastards ... Guess not that soft.

"I wanna' try that," said Peter's second looey.

"We're sitting here water-logged on a branch," said the boss pigeon, "and you want to pop out of the wet earth, soaking wet and muddy??"

"Looks like fun."

"Turning on a spit and cooking might be more fun."

"Sarcasm ... Right?"

"*We all need someone to lean on ... Someone toooooo* (really high note)... (then, really low note) ... *love!!*" The horde were spread throughout the trees, all soaking wet on their respective branches.

"Sarcasm ... Yes, sir."

"They're outta' hand ... you know?"

"You mean, 'outta' wing' ... Sir!!"

Boss Ant and his two lieutenants, already ass-landed, were water-logged and coughing as other ants kept shooting out of the hole---lotta' ants---spat out from their underground city in the muddy earth.

"All I was doing was eating some berries and drinking aphid milk---and what happens?" said Boss Ant. "I get spat out of the ground on a water slide---Who *built* the water slide?"

"That was no water slide, boss," said the first looey. "That was a design malfunction."

"Sarcasm," said the second looey.

"You mean," pondered Boss Ant, "no one built a water slide?"

"No," said the first looey.

"Certainly behaved like one."

"No," said the second looey.

"I really think it's a water slide," said Boss Ant.

"You do?" said the first looey.

"I'll get a detail on it for repairs and restructure ASAP," said the second looey.

"I like water slides," said Boss Ant.

"We almost drowned, sir," said the first looey.

"Yeah, that was fun."

"*Do it right next time---next time, -ime, -ime, -ime, -ime, -ime ...!!*" sang hundreds of thousands and maybe a million ... the ant mass, whatever.

"How is it they sound so similar to the pigeons?" said Boss Ant.

"Same campus and all those TVs and radios and podcasts and streams," said the first looey.

"I don't remember any streams, but I know where a swamp is."

"Yes, sir."

"It's a bit irritating."

"So is getting spat out of your own home."

"We need to get under a tree."

"A lot of birds up there," said the first looey.

"Lots of caca," said the second looey.

Boss Ant and the first looey stared at the second looey, no antennae necessary, perhaps thinking, *Between the giant raindrops and pigeon diarrhea---What do we do?*

"Potential: Lotta' shit … sir," said the first looey.

"How am I going to get millions of water-logged ants grouped under a tree?" said Boss Ant. "We talk with antennae, remember?"

Another lightning bolt snapped, crackled and burned nearby, this one splitting a boulder in two, a loud explosion, so loud, ringing ears again, even the tall grass flattened out with the stinging prickling vibrations, the rocks and stones and sand bounced and shifted, shooting out like shot bullets, debris; hardier birds in flight like the raptors and gulls spun around with the static, ionic stress everywhere, flight patterns dislodged, forgotten, some falling to the earth and water in disarray, confusion, and injured if not dead already from the shock of the lightning bolt.

After their shake-up and toss, the ants scrambled by the millions for the trees to hide under their roots that stuck out of the ground and climb the bark, whichever was closer. Their communication by antennae was uncanny, quick, and no one knew how they could be so organized.

They'd be better off climbing as high as they could.

The pigeons, shaken off their branches and flopped to the wet turf, managed to regroup in the trees. The ants, not much smaller than the flying caca-freaks, jammed themselves into crevices and over the bark, their antennae working feverishly, most of the communication amongst the millions of a shocked and shaken-up nature, and antennae phrases---"Holy crap!," "Just drown me, will ya'?," "Make some room, you're crowding me!," "The pigeons are up here!," and "Who invited them?"---were heard amongst other unprintable tenets of frustration and disapproval.

"You smell something?" said Peter.

"**Ants!!**" cried the water-logged pigeon horde.

"You smell something?" said Boss Ant.

"**Pigeons!!**" cried the water-logged ant mass.

"Ohhhh-oh sayyy can you seeee … myyyyyy eyes, if you can then you're too close to me!!" shout-sang the horde.

"**Up yours!!**" shouted the mass.

Hiccups could be heard everywhere from the horde and mass, sounding like crickets and katydids on speed. Water-logged stress.

"That's from T.V., huh?" said Peter.

"That and pod-casts … streaming … whatever," said the first looey.

"Did you fart?" said the pigeon first looey.

"**Maybe!!**" cried the ant mass.

Chapter 11: Convalescing Jamie & Back To The Berries & Another Campus Chase

The squall had stopped. It was muggy. Temperature: 85. Humidity: 100 percent---*soooo* muggy---summer. ...

In a jungle with a swamp on one side, college campus over there, and an encroaching suburb whose builders don't give a shit.

Then, there's Butts the squirrel, who rescued a black jaguar from a truck accident and knows where to find apples, snickers bars and acorns, and knows perfectly well how to lose 'em after he stashes 'em. Usually, he eats the snickers' peanuts ASAP.

He might lose his apples and acorns and dig in garbage cans, but he'd helped to create Pantherville. ...

Jamie sat forlornly in her home below the porch attached to the duplex suburban home.

"Would you like some apples, Jamie?" said Butts, who always felt he wasn't good enough for the lady raccoon except to fetch for her once in a while.

"Do you have any around here?"

"No. Campus."

"I don't want you to go all that way just for that."

"They're apples, not rocks," said the squirrel, rolling his eyes. "Besides, all I need to do is get the word out and they'll be here."

Jamie was exhausted, burnt out (lousy pun) and was projecting how she felt and the effort it would take for her to get the apples; right now, she could barely lift her eyelids.

"You shouldn't go to all that trouble."

"No trouble."

"How long have you two been getting along?" said Panther, who'd stepped up out of nowhere. The black jaguar was the personification of stealth. "Again."

"Where's Benja, your tag-along these days?" said Butts.

"He might be eating a lizard---or, two."

"Doesn't that go against a Pantherville edict or law---or something?"

"He doesn't like them, so he might as well eat them."

"You're kidding."

"I am."

"I thought you were getting me an apple," said Jamie.

"Right here," said Butts, who presented her with several slices of apple, all white with red skins.

"How'd you do that?!" said Panther.

Jamie just smiled and mouthed a "Thank you."

"He knows a few birds," said Kittay, another black jaguar who could similarly appear to just materialize---anywhere.

The apples appeared out of---nowhere.

"Thought you were out saving the world from lizards," said Butts. "*Big* lizards."

"You haven't been eaten, yet?" said Panther.

"I'm junk food, remember?"

"It's getting a little crowded for the house," said Jamie. "You might be seen."

"I've seen no sign of humans," said Panther.

"I've got an idea," said Butts. "I can take better care of her on the campus."

"I'm fine," said Jamie.

"No, you're not," said Panther---"and a good idea."

"I've always wanted to try those berries," said Kittay.

"Haven't you been to a Happy Hour?" said Butts.

"The campus berries aren't fermented---so I've heard."

"I *told* you that."

"So you did."

"You want more apples, you have to come by the campus."

"You telling me what to do?" said Jamie.

"Not me," said Panther.

"Not me," said Chipmunk.

"Not me," said Chimp.

"Not me," said William.

"Not me," said Amsterdam.

"Not me," said Nathaniel.

"Not me," said Brian.

They looked at Butts, who merely shrugged his shoulders.

"She's always mad at me about something," he said. "Might as well be this, too."

Cindy, Seysew, Robert, Rachel, Emily, Roberts, and Naja came crawling, traipsing (Really?), trampling (more like it), waddling and slithering along. Apparently, they didn't want to hang with the lizards.

Neither, the ants.

Not even the pigeons.

"Fine," said Jamie. "I'll go to the campus and eat berries and get real fat."

"Fart, too," said Chipmunk.

"Indeed," said Chimp.

"They don't make you fat," said Panther. "Just pee a lot."

"Fart, too," said Chipmunk.

"Shut up, dude," said Emily.

"They make me caca," said Benja.

"See?" said Chipmunk.

"You're nasty," said Rachel.

"Yeah, but I dump regularly."

"O.K., enough with the 'caca' talk," said Jamie.

"I wanna' try them," said Kittay, "and see what all the fuss is about."

"Farting!!" said Emily, Chimp, Rachel and Cindy, and probably a few others, too.

"See?" said Chipmunk.

Panther slapped his left paw over his eyes and sighed.

Elaine landed next to Nathaniel and Brian on the same log. Her wings kept flapping, damp from the recent storm.

"Knock it off!" said Brian.

"Flap somewhere else, hawk!" said Nathaniel.

"They're wet---I'm drying them off!"

"Are birds always so loud?" said Kittay.

Butts said, "We could have the pigeons meet the piranha before the fish get eaten by the lizards or Roberts before Benja realizes how good berries are and I don't have to put up with the pigeons anymore and Elaine stopped flapping her wings because they're dry now."

He took a breath. You'd have to stare. It's the only way.

Chipmunk recovered: "That would eliminate *two* problems. But the hawk will get wet again."

"A conundrum," said Rachel.

"There are so many, it seems," said Amsterdam, whom nothing seemed to bother. Nothing did. "Then again, Benja might not like berries."

"He already does," said Benja.

Where'd Benja …? Stealth.

"My bad," said Amsterdam.

"Whoopsie," said Panther. This time, he didn't slap a paw over his eyes.

"I haven't tried strawberries, yet," said Benja.

"Let's go get some berries so I can pee and poop," said Jamie.

"You get to fart, first," said Chipmunk.

"I don't think I said that," said Butts.

"I said 'pee'," said Panther.

"I said 'poop'," said Benja.

"I forget who's responsible," said Jamie.

"Someone said 'caca'," said Butts.

"Me," said Amsterdam. "I think."

On the campus and within the quad, students relaxed. Perhaps, they'd already peed and pooped, however the relaxation quotient they'd reached to get comfortable within their quad.

Butts the squirrel sat atop a plastic-lined 52-gallon garbage can just outside the campus cafeteria. He chewed on a zagnut or some other nutty bar, but it didn't appear to be a snickers. The wrapper wasn't familiar to the others, who were ensconced once again amongst the berry bushes---blueberries, raspberries, blackberries. No strawberries. Back toward the clearing, there were some bushes, but very few ate them.

Jamie pranced up to the garbage can. Perhaps, the students thought she might eat the squirrel, as she was making a lot of sound, chittering or chattering, while she looked toward up toward the smaller animal.

"This isn't good for you, Jamie," said Butts.

"I've been struck by lightning," she said. "I can eat anything I want. I'm indestructible."

"You're also really cute."

"Thank you."

She wasn't going to eat the squirrel. At least, the students didn't think so, but they appeared wary enough.

They didn't know that she'd rather kiss Butts. He didn't know, either.

"The berries are over here," said Panther, who figured correctly that the humans didn't understand the language of wild cat, nor would they suspect the various berry bushes and trees nearby of camouflaging many animals big and small.

Other beasts amongst the bushes and trees included a pygmy tarsier, a wolverine, a Bengal tiger, chimpanzee, angora cat, panda bear, huge alligator, even bigger African elephant, blind-as-a-bat gorilla, two snakes of considerable size, one bigger than the other.

No ants.

No pigeons.

No clams.

No piranha.

There were three birds in the air, a red-tail hawk, crow and raven. They didn't seem too interested in snickers bars, co-eds, or berries. But, show a shiny wrapper, and they might change their flight patterns.

A low-slung cloud appeared in the distance, off-white with so many black dots, might've been dust, debris … eyes, and like a huge hoard of locusts, a throng of pigeons flight-stumbled their way toward the campus.

Butts looked up from Jamie and over his shoulder, as Elaine, Brian, and Nathaniel landed and perched on the 52-gallon plastic-lined rim opposite.

"How can I help you?"

The birds stared at the squirrel, then flopped into the mass----mess---of delicacies.

The garbage can was surrounded by thousands, millions---uncountable ants. Perhaps, they'd spell out "Ant Music" or "Them!" or whatever they considered a celebration of their existence; however irritating they were, more so than the pigeons (not really) or lizards (eh).

"Just what do you think you're doing down there?" shouted Butts into the din.

"*In* here," said one of the birds; it was hard to tell which one with the plastic-lined and goopy-garbage acoustics.

"Whatever! This is *my* mess of stash!"

"'Stash'!"

"Don't mimic me, bird---whichever of you said that!"

"It was me!"

"No … Me!"

"*Meeeee*!!"

"Dang it, why don't you go eat the berries like everyone else does!!"

"Dude, calm down."

"What?!" Butts spun back around on his perch on the 52-gallon can and---Voila! It was Chipmunk.

"Ohhhh, c'mon, not you, too!"

"Chill, boss."

"Yeah, yeah, yeah, go get your berries like the rest of 'em."

"It's not your campus---or, your quad, your co-eds, your garbage can."

"You didn't get the memo, huh?"

"What's a 'memo'?"

"You know how long I've been coming here?"

"Does it matter?"

"What do you mean?"

"I don't see your name anywhere around here."

In the bushes and amongst the trees, there were too many beasties---Panther, Benja, Amsterdam, Rachel, Emily, Chimp, coupla' big snakes, Cindy, Seysew, an alligator, pygmy tarsier (up there, hangin' from a branch ... twig ...), and Kittay.

Seysew, who hung back on the outskirts of the jungle, looked down at her feet.

"Oh ... you're here."

Kinle and the other Komodos were settled closer to the forest floor than the African elephant would ever want to be---at least when the lizards were already there. They were poisonous: don't tempt the buggers.

The ants ... not yet.

The pigeons landed as haphazardly as they could along the cement walkway and grassy knolls as students from many walks-of-life and studies scattered, some yelling *"Heyyyy!!"* or screeching *"Yeeee!!"* or *"Help! Save us!!"* or "What the ****?!" and other stuff of surprise and protest that may or may not have fit the problem (well, bird shit stinks) or crisis (potential: lotta' birds, lotta' shit) at hand ... or foot ... arm ... shoes and socks ... so many sandals and bare-footin', not too many socks.

"Why?" said Panther.

"Why ... What?" said Benja.

"You can't eat them because they taste like caca."

"I'd rather eat my own boogers."

"Don't you, anyway?"

"That was gross," said Jamie as she chomped a few blueberries.

"These are damn good," said Kittay as she chewed a few raspberries.

Pigeons: falling over themselves, tripping into each other. The ants (yeah, they're here) held their ground, or sidewalk, as they bit away at the caca-birds, a nasty business; the birds received the business-end of too-many-to-count tiny bites. It was a free-for-all, a fiasco, a conundrum---co-eds running for their lives!

Not really.

But, it was …

Ants vs. pigeons: revisited.

The co-eds managed to scamper around and through the morass of black-eyed poopers, still holding their textbooks, drinks, smart phones, backpacks on their backs, no bras (don't choke again on the berries, big cats) and---"*Eeeuuuuu!*" and "*Gross!*" and "*Ohhh … my … God!*"---and Butts surveyed the scene while Chipmunk crouched next to him and three birds resurfaced from the innards of the 52-gallon plastic-lined garbage can and clutched with their sharp claws the rim opposite the forest rodents, flapping their wings for balance, claws also clutching messy goodies from within the barrel.

So many ants: Pigeons let out cries of pain and irritation---"*Cut* that out!" "You little *bastard*!" "Son of a *bitch*!"

"The neighborhood's getting really crowded," said Butts, as he crunched through another zagnut. He wasn't sure now which one he liked more: zagnut or snickers ... tough call.

"Kinda' noisy on campus today," said Jamie in an understatement as she licked her paws clean of berry juice. Yummy.

"I just feel that something really stupid or goofy---no, just stupid---is about to happen," said Amsterdam.

"Kinda' prescient, that thinking," said Chimp, who scratched himself. He's a guy.

"I think I wanna' get back to the clearing," said Roberts.

"You don't eat fruit, dude," said Emily.

"Gotta' be quieter there than here," said Cindy.

"Why are we here?" said Rachel.

"Getting away from the lizard population," said William, still hanging out. Check that twig.

"Didn't work," said Kinle.

"I knew you were there. I was hoping you'd disappear."

"You lizards stink," said Seysew.

"You fart, too, elephant," said Kinle.

Butts saw a gleaming wrapper on top of the latest mound of waste below him in the depths of "his" garbage can.

"Ah, ha!" he yelled and leapt within.

Jamie burped. "Excuse me," she said.

"Feeling better?" said Emily.

"I guess so."

Butts grabbed the prize in his jaw. He leapt back up to the rim.

"Why'd I listen to you two?" said Elaine.

"Because you thrive on adventure," said Nathaniel.

"Because you're an idiot," said Brian.

"*Mmgftttgagr Briamph*," said Butts.

"What?!" said Elaine.

"He said that he agrees with the raven---you know, the bigger ugly-azz black bird," said Chipmunk.

"Hey!" cried the smaller of the two black birds.

"Hey!!" cried the bigger of the two black birds.

"Stay away from me or I'll *bite* you!"

"*Mmwttchhh ott bvvvvrds, chee mffeenzzit,*" said Butts.

Squirrel, you're drooling, dude.

"What'd he say that time?" said Elaine.

"He said, 'Watch out birds, he means it,'" said Chipmunk. "He means *me*."

Peter and the pigeons stepped back from the ants while the co-eds whoopsie-daisied back and forth, their manicured fingernails over their mouths of "Oh"s, lip-gloss shiny under partly cloudy skies, hot and humid, white tank tops, two brunettes, one redhead, so many sun freckles.

Panther choked on some blackberries.

Benja choked on some raspberries.

"You two are disgusting," said Cindy.

"We're *guys*!" said Benja.

"They got that right," said Amsterdam, who somehow knew what was going on, his sense of smell and hearing on full alert, although he had no idea the tank tops were white but that didn't matter in his imagination, which was aided and abetted by his other senses.

"They may be disgusting," said Emily, "but at least they're honest about it."

Butts leapt from the rim of the garbage again.

Panther put his right paw over his eyes.

Amsterdam laughed.

The co-eds laughed so hard they farted, one after the other. Glorious.

No one wanted the pigeons to fart. That might be disastrous.

Butts cleared the pigeons and ants in a couple of hops, then went through the legs of all three co-eds---

"*Eeeeeek!*"

"*Whoopsie!*"

"*Daisie!*"

---zig-zagging, and found himself at the bushes panting and with a half-eaten snickers stuck in his jaw.

The crow, raven and red-tail took off and gave chase after him. The Shiny-Wrapper Syndrome, again; otherwise known as the Shiny Wrapper Chase.

Panther stared at him through the bushes. That's all Butts could see: The big cat's green (daytime) eyes---the *smaller* big cat's eyes.

"*Mmfggshabammmftghh!*" said the squirrel. That meant … *What?*

Drool *Drool* *Drool*

"You got three huge birds after you."

"*Nfftnmmghwtch!*" Got it! That meant … *Not on my watch*! He took off, scampering back in the opposite direction.

Co-eds, ants, pigeons, and a chipmunk, still up there on the rim---all confused---and three big-azz birds turned direction mid-flight.

That way ... Butts shifted and scampered over there, his tail twitching, sounding a protest, anger, heading up the sidewalk, birds shifting again and giving chase---yeah, they're attracted to shiny stuff---because it had nothing to do with the candy bar, nope.

The other animals watched and ate berries. Yummm.

Except ... Snakes don't eat berries, but they do eat the creatures eating the berries, just like other carnivores.

They leave the elephant alone---too big.

They leave the jaguars and tiger alone---too dangerous.

Amsterdam would twist them into a pretzel.

Ouch.

The lizards didn't eat berries, either, but the snakes didn't care about them; perhaps, too big, too.

Meanwhile ... Butts tripped over a stump and went not-quite-literally flying, but he was airborne, landed face-first, choking on the wrapper, which he inadvertently tried to swallow.

Ptooey!!

The half-eaten snickers with its shiny wrapper landed over there, loaded with squirrel spit, just behind four co-eds sitting on a blanket and sharing a Cheez-It box and each drinking a Red Bull or Green Giant (not) or orange roughy (What?!) or white lightnin' (maybe) ...

Butts ran over to the berry bushes and spoke into them, looking kind of stupid. He is a squirrel.

Mean.

Pandemonium ... Co-eds (again) *"Eeeeek!"*ing and *"Eeeeeuuu!"*ing and stuff like that, scampering much like the squirrel to all points of the compass ... campus.

"I need you, big guy."

Which one?

"No," said Panther.

Butts looked toward Benja, hidden away in a deeper thicket.

"I need you, big guy."

"You're kidding."

Chipmunk couldn't stop laughing from atop the 52-gallon garbage can. To the co-eds, his laughter sounded like the world's tiniest dolphin (about six inches long) trying to warn everyone while trailing backwards above the waterline about an incoming tidal wave.

Three co-eds remained sitting on the grass where they'd been tripped up. They had no urge to get up and get tripped again. At least, they hadn't a saliva-spewed half-eaten snickers bar spat in their direction, like the Cheez-It girls.

Brian, Nathaniel, and Elaine landed on a log again not far from the berry bushes.

To the others, even the human kind of creature, it must have looked bizarre: A hawk, crow, and raven perched side by side---but not any more than a squirrel doing a steeplechase with a gooey snickers.

Another example: Big-azz wild cats eating berries.

The pigeons juked and jived and were juxta-positioned near and around the fallen snickers.

The ants formed a bridge with their own bodies and, like a slinky, landed on top the leftover candy bar and its ripped and shiny wrapper. With their landing, the shine could no longer be seen.

Butts had returned to the rim alongside Chipmunk.

Nathaniel, Brian and Elaine flew back and again landed alongside the two forest rodents.

"I fail," said Elaine, "to see the thrill in this---"

"Who asked you??" spat Butts.

"---now."

"We'll check the schedule and let you know when it gets exciting again," said Chipmunk.

"We like shiny things," said Brian.

"I like to eat!!" yelled Butts.

"Berries, right over here," said Jamie as she chewed away on some raspberries.

Panther growled from within the bushes---*Is it Happy Hour yet? Why do I feel responsible? Maybe the ants will get eaten by the pigeons get eaten by the hawk get eaten by the gator get stomped by the elephant get run over by a hurricane ... Then, I can take a nap after that.*

Mean. Really silly, too---plus: highly improbable.

Heck with this! thought Butts. He scampered back toward the mosh-pit of ants and pigeons, leaping over the sedentary co-eds (the Cheez-It girls ... wait, maybe not) in the process---

"Squirrel!"

"Squirrel!"

"We love you!"

---and bull-dozed his way through the pigeons to the wall of ants covering the shiny stuff.

"Gutsy," said Panther.

"Ballsy," said Benja.

"That's my squirrel," said Jamie.

"Really?!" said Amsterdam.

"**Move!!**" yelled Butts.

The ant mass---so many *millions* of eyes---stared at him, their antennae communicating at the most rapid of paces---"That *furry creature is friggin'* **NUTS!!**"

"I'd rather be at a picnic!" yelled Boss Ant.

"This *sucks!*" yelled the first looey.

"Big Time!" yelled the second looey.

"*I'm onnn my way---I'm making iiiit!!*" sang the ant mass.

"I am *not* figuring *that* one out!" yelled Boss Ant.

"**Move!!**" The squirrel's tail flipped several times. It was anger.

The ants moved, shifted, jumped, did backflips, flashed birdies (that can mean two things---one's impossible, the other improbable), careened this way and that, and crashed into each other and the garbage can's outer wall. The squirrel grabbed the snickers and departed, stage right, left, whatever---*that* way.

He sideswiped about 20 pigeons.

"*Whip them good!!* ... *Do do do do do!!*" sang the ant mass.

"Just like that?" said Peter.

"I don't even like snickers!" yelled the first looey.

"I'd rather eat bread crumbs," said the second looey, not so loud.

"*Do wah diddy diddy dum diddy do*!!" sang the pigeon horde.

"What they said," mused Peter. "None of this makes sense."

"What's supposed to make sense?" said the first looey.

"Yeah, we're pigeons," said the second looey.

"All we're supposed to care about and make sense of is making babies, scavenging in parks and on campus quads; taking off, flying, and landing off-balance sober or not; dumping caca; and having the brain-wave potential of a gnat."

"That was harsh," said Peter.

"Don't forget about getting into arguments with ants," said the second looey.

"Gnats, ants, piranhas, clams ... *so* much skullduggery," said the first looey.

"You're comparing us to gnats?" said Peter.

"A bit of an exaggeration, yes."

Butts ran full speed toward the bushes, the shiny wrapper flapping in the breeze. The candy bar was loaded with squirrel drool. It wasn't as gross as when he fell into the garbage can a while back, but it was still pretty icky. The drool may have kept the ants from being too curious in the brief time they surrounded the prized possession.

"You're drooling," said Jamie, who had her share of berry juice on her lips and cheeks.

"*Wrrrthhchhhittt,*" said the squirrel, his mouth clamped. He continued to breathe hard as he tried to sit still a moment after scampering for the most part the last 10 minutes or so.

"I think I know what he said," said Benja. "But, I'm not sure."

Three birds, a crow, raven, and red-tail hawk came swooping down towards the shiny wrapper.

"This is a game, right?" said Nathaniel, his claws extended.

"*Wvvvutzatallzzzeryorshvisss---mmkkoopp*?" said Butts, mumbling and drooling, leading an all-star campus performance, as he readied to run again---the other way.

"I got it!" said Benja. "He said, 'What's that all over your face---make-up'!"

The squirrel raised his eyebrows.

"What's 'make-up'?" said William.

"Human stuff," said Emily. She had berry juice on her whiskered face, too.

"Now where you going?" said Jamie.

"*Iiiivzohhhdeyyyaaaa!*" said the squirrel, as his mumbling and marble-y voice went Doppler moving off to the right, the shiny-wrapped drool-draped snickers flapping away as he scampered off into the forest's trees. The three birds shifted in flight, retracting their claws. The game wasn't as much fun in the jungle; much too difficult to track.

They were tired of translating drool-talk.

"I do not feel responsible," said Panther.

"Only if you're an idiot," said Benja, who lumbered off into the same jungle.

Chapter 12: How Cheap The Rotting Fruit, Part II:

Return Of The Souse

Behold: Sunshine with approaching cumulus clouds, nimbus status (or stratus) their imminence, because the Everglades and its Pantherville must have several storm cells each day in the summer, and the next one might give Happy Hour a shower.

It's gonna' get wet.

They'll be happily soused, again, and won't care about getting wet.

"Back from the hunt, big guy?" said Butts.

"I ate," said Panther.

"Did it taste like chicken?"

"What?"

"Never mind."

Jamie ambled into the clearing and sat up against a tree and sighed.

"The last time you did that you got zapped."

"Squirrel, have some tact," said Amsterdam.

The blind gorilla was over there sitting against a kapok. He scratched himself in the nether region.

"You gotta' do that here?!" said Butts.

"I can't help it you don't have much of a package," said the silverback.

"It's kind of *relative*, isn't it??"

Panther and Benja both laughed; that guttural big-cat laughter, scary, ominous, like they're about to kill something.

Other creatures great and small made their way to the ripe and rotting fruits; even the Komodos were welcome. Of course, after a few chunky, chewy and juicy cocktails, no one cared who was there: Come one come all … *hiccup* …

The sky darkened to the west, but it wasn't a storm. The huge shadow was close to the treetops; circulating and circumnavigating amongst the trees.

Pigeons. Again. Locusts are supposed to do this.

Fruit makes you crap … lotta' fruit at Happy Hour … here come the pigeons.

Damn. Shit.

The only beasties not in the clearing might've been the piranha. Perhaps, someone should grab a wading pool.

Panther said to Kinle, "Did you eat?"

"Yeah, we found some grub."

"'Grubs'?"

"Never mind."

"Damn birds!" said Nathaniel. He and Brian had just landed on a scrub pine branch. Elaine landed on the ground.

"Oh, c'mon!" said Chipmunk. "I'm not drunk enough, yet!"

"It's *them*!" Brian pointed with a wing toward the incoming white mass of feathers, black eyes, and klutzy flight patterns. They were here again for Happy Hour and no one wanted to guess how they'd fly away afterward, after their satiation and saturation of fruit and its fermentation.

"They really need to stay as sober as possible," said Amsterdam.

"Not on my watch," said Rachel.

"Mine, either," said Emily.

"Nor mine," said Chimp.

"How boring," said Cindy.

"Agreed," said Panther as he snarfed a ripe mango.

"I'd like to see that," said Butts.

"What?"

"Any of you on your *watch* keeping hundreds of flying vermin from getting fruit-soused."

"It doesn't matter if they eat the fruit or not," said Amsterdam. "They fly funny, anyway."

"And shit."

"It's a shame no one wants to eat them," said Benja, "but they're probably about as fatty as a squirrel."

"Hey!" said Butts. He belched after swallowing some bits of apple.

"Is it my turn to eat some piranha?" said Roberts. He swallowed three mangos at once and belched, much louder than the squirrel.

"Bunch of pigs," said Robert as he hung from a kapok limb. He swallowed an apple whole. It was almost purple, definitely overripe. He belched, louder than Roberts.

"Hey!" said the gator.

"Burping's good for you," said Naja, who also hung from a limb, a gum tree. She snarfed a few blueberries. She belched, louder than the squirrel, but not as loud as Robert, but maybe louder than Roberts. It was hard to be sure.

"All of you---hypocrites!" cried Butts.

"Shut up and go run a campus, squirrel," laughed Panther. Then, he hiccupped. "Dammit'." No one likes hiccups.

Fermenting fruit was an acquired taste for the carnivores; even some of the herbivores and worth it for the belching and farting, but not the hiccups.

The pigeons fell through several pine trees. That had to hurt.

Ants right below one of the trees. It must've been planned.

"They've not one bit of fruit, yet," said Amsterdam, shaking his huge head.

Many cries of pain and cursing as hundreds of them bumped and ricocheted from the branches, all of them falling to the ground, some of them actually landing on their feet, but mostly, plopping down on their heads and tushies.

Well, they're here.

"I think they do it on purpose," said Chipmunk.

"'Tis an entrance," said Jamie.

"I don't think they crap by accident, either," said Amsterdam, who hadn't eaten anything. There were coconuts on the beach. No one was sure if they were his food and nourishment of choice. No one ever saw him eat. He was about profundity and kicking giant lizards' asses. He was Zen.

The ants scattered here and there and then reconvened to confront the klutzy pigeons, however klutzy they really were. It could've been a ploy. They might've enjoyed crappin' on everyone's heads ... Life: Figured out.

Panther didn't think they were smart or strong enough to control themselves, control their bowels. He shuddered. *Thank goodness for that thunderstorm.* Trying to get to the bay took a while. The big cat shuddered again as he remembered that mess and the stink. It never really bothered him, or Benja, but the others …

"You should drop in more often---not!!" yelled Boss Ant.

"You seem to think you're the most popular beast besides the *cockroach*---Ha!!" cried Peter the leader. "Neither of you are!!"

"We got here first!"

"You're a bigger pain in the tush than the cockroach, too!"

"That's debatable," said Jamie.

"*Let's all have a cockamamie good tyyyme*!!" screeched the ant mass and pigeon horde together.

"O.K., that was weird," said both first looeys.

"O.K., that *was* weird," said Butts. He was eating a raspberry.

"Lots of volume," said Panther as he sighed.

"Loud," said Benja.

"They're probably around each other more than we care to know."

"We don't 'care' that they're here," said Rachel, "and wish they were elsewhere."

The pigeons bobbed and babbled their way past the ants, whose pincers readied to bite but they didn't.

"*Berries*!!" yelled both scrums. "*Yum, yum, eeeeeat 'em up*!!"

"It a lightning bolt came down and hit them," said Chimp, "Would we have to worry about it?"

"Don't go there," said Jamie. She shivered with the memory.

"Lightning bolt hits them," said Amsterdam, "it hits us, too. Trust me on this."

"So, we're going there?"

"Sorry."

Panther slapped his right paw over his eyes.

"Mosquito?" said Benja.

"Frustration."

"Get a headache hitting yourself like that."

"Considered."

Pantherville's beasties backed off as two of the three least-welcome (other: giant lizards) groups of animals raced to the fruity bushes consisting of blackberries, blueberries, raspberries, strawberries---but no cherries or boysenberries, oh well.

"You could just crush them, couldn't you, Seysew?" said Chimp.

"The berries?" said Seysew.

Uh uh.

"*Eeeuuuuu ...*" said Emily.

"Gross," said Jamie.

"Sicko," said Rachel.

"Blech," said Cindy.

"I don't want to get my feet dirty," said the elephant.

"Nasty," said Amsterdam.

No, Chimp hadn't meant the berries.

"We either have stew or wine," said William, "depends on what you step on."

C'mon …

"Gross," said Jamie.

"*Eeeeuuuu* …" said Emily.

"Sicko," said Rachel.

"Blech," said Cindy.

"*Nasty*," said Amsterdam.

"You might wanna' slap your face again," said Benja to Panther.

"Try it, you might like it."

The Bengal slapped his own face with his right paw.

"Kinda' stupid … hurts, too." Benja blinked several times.

"Next time, close your eyes." Panther grinned.

The pigeons formed a ring about 10 birds thick around the ants. How they organized that way only they knew; they couldn't take off or land with any precision, so maybe the pull of the moon had something to do with this.

The other animals were stunned.

"How'd they do that?!" said Panther.

"Bless their geometric souls," said the gorilla. His sense of movement and its detection was very keen.

"I'll bet they have no idea what they're doing," said Chimp.

"At least they don't scratch themselves like you," said Emily.

"Hey!" said Chimp and Amsterdam and William, primates all.

"Could've been a square," said Chipmunk.

"Who gives a shit?" said Cindy.

"I don't, do you?" said Panther. He glanced at Benja.

"Nope." He chewed up and swallowed a whole mango. ...*Gulp*... He'd done this before.

"That's at least two fruits you like, Benja boy," said Jamie.

"That's right."

"'Benja boy'?" said Panther.

"Who am I to argue?"

"Why are you here?" said Peter.

"Why are *you* here?" said Boss Ant.

"We could just stomp you," said the pigeon first looey.

"You're not big enough!" exclaimed the ant first looey.

"We could peck you into submission," said the pigeon second looey.

"We could bite you all day!" exclaimed the ant second looey.

"Jack and Jill went up the hill---!!" sang the pigeon horde.

"---To fetch a pail of wahhhh-ter!!" sang the ant mass, in much higher voices, pinched, rather.

"Eerie," said Jamie.

"To say the least," said Emily. Both of them were walking crooked. Happy Hour and its fermented fruits took a toll, a wonderful price to pay; Vitamin-C and getting plastered--- free.

"Why are they singing the same song?" said Boss Ant.

"Why are they singing the same song?" said Peter.

Pigeons and ants stared at each other. So many ... Eat some fruit, boys.

The bay's surface sparkled in the late afternoon sun. Not one but two swirling shifting spinning pods of piranha swam parallel to each other, and just like the ants and pigeons singing the same song, explaining how the piranha swarms could be swimming in unison was something that, similar to the pigeon horde and ant mass, perhaps only the piranha could explain.

"How do you show up every time we show up?" said Peter.

"You accusing us of stalking you?" said Boss Ant.

"If the shoe fits!"

"What's a 'shoe'?"

"It's when you tell someone to go *away*---Shoo!"

Boss Ant looked at his lieutenants, who shrugged (yeah, ants can shrug … whatever). He looked back at the mass of ants---*they* shrugged in unison. Pretty cool shit.

"I guess you're full of caca in more ways than one!" said Boss Ant.

"What does *that* mean?" said Peter.

"Means shove it up your *arse*, caca-breath!"

"*I'm gonna' wash that man right out of my hair*!!" sang the pigeon horde and ant mass.

"What?!" exclaimed Boss Ant.

"You guys spend *wayyy* too much time on campus!" exclaimed Peter. Whether he directed this comment at both the mass of ants and horde of pigeons---it was hard to tell.

"Your birds are a bad influence on my ants!"

"Your ants are a bad influence on my birds!"

"They're singing a Broadway tune---hardly a bad influence," said Amsterdam.

"What's a 'Broadway'?" said Roberts.

"Human stuff, and between myself, the squirrel, pigeons, raccoon and ants there's certainly been enough interaction."

"What about Panther and Benja?" said Emily.

"I need to scratch myself," said Chimp, "but I'm waiting for Amsterdam to do it, first."

"Thank you for that info," said Cindy. "May I barf?"

"Any mangos left?" said Kinle. He and the other lizards remained on the fringe of the clearing.

"On the beach," said Panther. "Coconuts are there, too."

"Yeah, but they're not overly ripe."

"Do they have to be?"

"No."

"Learn to like apples or raspberries or---"

"Some mangos over here," said Jamie.

"---Never mind. My bad. Go get soused."

"*Shake it up, baby, twist and shout*!!" the horde and mass sang together.

"Millions of ants and hundreds of pigeons singing a song from the 1950's," said Amsterdam. "Amazing."

"I'm going to the beach to see the sunset," said Panther.

"I'll join you," said Benja.

"I'm going for the peace and quiet."

"I won't say a word."

"*Awwwwwww, freak out … le chic … le freak … freak out*!!!"

"You can't eat 'em," said Benja.

"Be sick for days," said Panther.

"Hey, piranha!" said Kinle.

Both big cats thought, *Ohhh, crap*!!

"My piranha!!" exclaimed Roberts.

"Since when?"

"Piranha!" yelled Peter.

"Good," said Boss Ant. "Go get eaten."

"They won't eat us; too much fat."

"They can't *see* us."

"You're full of crap!"

"*You're* full of crap!"

"**LET'S ALL CRAP!!**" cried the horde and mass.

"That's scary," Peter said.

"Your fault," said Boss Ant.

"What?!"

"Just kidding."

"Happy Hour will finish in peace," said Amsterdam. "Now, I shall go to the beach, too, where the piranha will have a choice of drunken delicacies."

"That's mean," said Jamie. "But, the fish won't be around long, either." She took after the big cats, who weren't about to chase down the lizards, those loonies, and Roberts, who was bigger than anyone except Seysew.

Everyone ducked for cover as Peter and his several-hundred-fold clan took and gained altitude, not much---scaring the bushes and trees in all their clumsiness, bumping and ramming each other, no sense of direction but, they flew and kept flying, however haphazardly. They might've been saving their caca for the fishies. Only they knew for sure. Then again, maybe they didn't.

Komodos raced over the tundra, dampened from the most recent storm, which occurred hours ago, so the bay was due to light up again, soon, at some point, with lightning, but no one really cared. Don't tell Jamie that. She's still sore.

The piranha might already be toasted when the lizards get there.

Roberts trailed them by just yards. That big-azz dinosaur could move. He was hungry, too. Don't take his piranha!

No thunder, yet.

"By the time we get there, it might be stormy and those idiots can't be that stupid," said Panther.

"Might be more food for me and you," said Benja.

"I wouldn't mind eating barbeque."

"Indeed."

There was the bay, sparkling in the dusk. The setting sun, in and out all day (a typical summer day in the tropical 'Glades), gave the sparkling bay an ethereal and supernatural quality.

Heeerrrrre, fishy fishy fishies ...

They zoomed in from the jungle, hanging from vines, jumping over rocks, roots and avoiding overhanging twigs and branches and spider webs---"*Ptooey!*" *Gag* "I think I *swallowed* one!" *Spit* *Spit* *Spit*---over pebbles, then coarse sand and, finally, the fine white coastal "dirt" that was broken shell.

The animals loomed through the trees and along the path, zigzagged and zoomed, crawling and flying, going fast enough; and they zeroed in on whatever it was they counted on---food, sunset, settling for sleep. Here they were, whatever their marks, footprints, flight patterns, destinations, the final pages of the final chapter of this story.

Don't worry about the piranha. There are more.

Here they come: pigeons---*zzzoooooooooommmm*!!!---flapped their clumsy selves over the beachhead, Komodos trampled over the sand, and Roberts, all 15 feet of him and still spitting out a spider or two, and Amsterdam, that Zen dude, who's been chuckling for at least the last 10 to 15 minutes, because no one wants to prove how funny life is when your hearing becomes acute with sight unseeing. (Thank you, Amsterdam.)

Panther and Benja came along with Kittay, who'd done most of the hunting back by the swamp lately for the black jaguar and the Bengal; then again, she was really good at it. More often than not, lady cats do the hunting and fishing.

Cindy, Rachel, Butts, Jamie, Chimp, Chipmunk, and Emily weren't far behind.

Seysew took her time. The beaten-down path wasn't made for her. She had to be careful to avoid breaking branches and limbs. She was big and she was strong.

The sunset attracted a lot of attention. No one wanted to miss it this time. With all the summer thunderstorms in these parts, tonight it was clear, and the setting sun could be seen. Let's not miss it.

The ants and snakes remained back at the clearing. Robert and Naja had eaten, or swallowed (depending on the perspective), and they were digesting or ingesting (again depending on the perspective).

The swamp and its surrounds: Good to the carnivores, as prescribed (ordered) by Panther and Benja.

The ants: They're fast, but not big enough to get anywhere fast enough, so they'd wait for the pigeons to get back so they can irritate the shit out of them again.

Seysew stopped the ground from shaking as she stopped stomping (walking) the ground at the front of the jungle nearest the sand. That's as far as she went. Sand: bad news for pachyderms.

"I don't have any desire to hunt a piranha," said William. He was on top of the elephant's head. There were bits of mango all over him. He didn't care. Next thunderstorm: He'd clean up.

Sunset: Soon.

Roberts and the lizards leapt into the low waves of the bay at the same time. The piranha, consisting of two rotating balls of sharp-toothed fury, shifted and headed back whence they came, wherever that was. The gator's and monitors' leaps found them splashing with resentment into several feet of water---no fish.

"What just happened?" said Roberts, who was about to foam at the mouth. He was pissed.

"They're going the other way, stupid---er, big guy, dinosaur, gator thingy," said Butts.

"See them!" exclaimed Kinle, as a dozen monitors jumped through the water, headed for their next meal.

"No, you don't!" said Roberts as he cursed---"Damn!"---and chased after the smaller lizards.

"Mouth!" yelled Jamie. She sat on a sand dune with Butts, Rachel, Emily, Chimp, and Chipmunk.

"Sorry!" yelled the gator. *What did I say? Oh, yeah ...*

Pigeons flew out over the water and managed to entangle themselves amongst themselves---they're *good* for that---quite a few losing a feather as they rammed each other, falling to the low-breaking waves, hitting the water---*Plop* *Plop* *Plop*---*fizzzzzzz* as the two spinning mounds of piranha about-faced (once) again, the lizards and gator splashing careening by, too fast---*Snap* *Snap* *Snap* *Snap*---jaws crackling popping empty air and water; klutzy winged caca birds struggling to fly away off the low waves---"Missed me!" "Ha!" "Get away!" "We taste like caca---Remember?"---the piranha didn't care; a frenzied ball of carnivorous sharp-toothed fishies snapped their jaws on air and water.

So much ... grunting.

Cursing---"Mouths!!"

Farting---"Not the pigeons---*Please*!!"

Caca birds finally flew up and away from the water, close calls (piranhas will eat anything, even caca birds), rejoining their brethren who'd managed not to klutz themselves into the waves.

It has been established in this story---Pigeons: not too smart.

Then again, they never get shat upon.

The bay's water remained turbulent as the various beasts jockeyed for position, to eat or be eaten, get out of the way, escape, the piranha and pigeons and lizards and gator in a cat's cradle of survival and hunting; most everyone else watched in amazement, while several tried not to laugh too hard---Amsterdam, Panther and Benja.

Like a tennis match, and as spectators, the animals' eyes went back and forth as the piranha, monitors, Roberts and the pigeons shifted left and right, back and forth, the pigeons just above the waterline, some bouncing off the scaly rough backs of the dinosaurs, the Komodos and the gator, in the water. The birds might have thought they could land there---"there" on the backs of dinosaurs.

Sun set: A cloud bank to the left, creeping, 30 miles from the beach and its cacophony, activity, frenetic, splashing, cursing, a few farts and heavy breathing, heaving---featured scattered lightning bolts every few seconds way out there, another storm cell in summer's daily one-two punch of squalls, animals perhaps confused, the gator and lizards looking just as goofy and exhausted as the pigeon, with nothing to do but chase after these fish, like there's nothing else to eat, just more fish and other game back by the swamp and its surrounds.

"Do they realize there're more fish in the swamp?" said Chipmunk, who also sat on Seysew's head. William and Chipmunk looked like pimples up there. It was hard to see either of them, although one was a bit bigger than the other.

Not really.

"I think I ate too many overripe mangos," said William. "I see mermaids."

"Those are manatees," said Amsterdam. "You can tell the difference because they're not nearly as pretty as mermaids."

"You spent a lot of time around humans, didn't you?" said Panther.

"Wish they'd been mermaids."

"There're no such things as mermaids," said Chipmunk.

"I don't think humans realize that."

"I think humans refuse to realize that," said Benja.

"Sometimes, humans make these pigeons look pretty damn smart."

"They're making their aggressors look kinda' stupid right now."

"You mean the fish, right?"

"The fish are making fools of them, too."

The pigeons ducked and weaved, showing abilities, and seemed to be enjoying themselves. The gator snapped away at empty water and air, clamping his huge toothy jaws on nothing, and the monitors jumped back and forth trying to avoid Roberts' tail---who probably didn't care what he ate he was so hungry---and occasionally a Komodo landed several yards away in the water or on the beach after getting wacked by the tail, only to scramble back to the fray, leaping splashing diving. It was no longer about the piranha: They could not be seen. Perhaps, they'd swum out deeper and emboldened to break up their spinning structures in the name of survival.

Hey, they taste good.

"Should we tell the boys?" said Jamie.

"What?" said Butts.

"That they look really stupid right now," said Rachel.

"You tellin' a gator that??" said Emily.

"Not," said Chimp.

Cindy, Emily and Chimp were chewing on clam meat, raw and gummy and delicious. Jamie joined them.

"Thanks, Panther," all four said in unison.

When? Oh, nevermind.

Kittay sat next to Panther on the sand. Benja eyed them both. He knew a good thing when he saw one, no matter how long they'd been away from each other. He saw another couple in Butts and Jamie and noticed that the squirrel always managed to be in the vicinity of the raccoon and vice-versa.

Amsterdam, mused the Bengal, also knew this stuff because *that blind gorilla can "see" everything*, perhaps even the future. His perceptual skill-set needed no help from his lost eyesight. But, *I'm sure he misses his eyes.*

The sun, now below the horizon, gave off its mauves and purples, its receding glow reacting with the atmospheres of planet Earth. The incoming storm, at least an hour away, appeared closer than it was with the backlighting available from the sun's afterglow. Streaks of lightning seemed to last longer, but it was only the imprint of the frequent bolts' reflections on the cornea of the various sets of eyes in Pantherville. When Panther, Jamie and Butts and the others looked away, the jagged lightning remained an outline or imprint over everything they looked at, even each other.

So ... Panther, there's a lightning bolt running through your tummy ... cool.

William relaxed under the branch of a coconut palm. He hung there by his prehensile tail. He was chillin'---mango messy---but chillin'. A full moon shone through the trees, not quite in the opposite direction, a bit north-northeast from the mauve and purple sky of the sunset, which was going purple-black, another storm cell with its lightning brigade-of-light, looming. The moon reflected in its dimmer dusk light from the eyes of the pygmy tarsier hanging upside down from the branch of the coconut palm; imagine how bright those big eyes would glow in the next hour or so as the full moon went bright, before and after the incoming storm. The littlest primate was sticky from mango, but thundershowers were on their way.

It's hard catching fish that don't wanna' be caught. The piranha had learned. If pigeons were fish, the world would have so much food.

Nope. Pigeons, whether fish or fly, taste like caca.

The piranhas' swirling twin-bill had reformed down the beach. There, they'd meander back up, eating other smaller fish along the way, along with other sea-going and land-moving creatures unfortunate. By then, the other beasts of prey might be asleep or too exhausted to tackle *any* fish in the waves. Plus: another storm.

The smart ones hunted back by the swamp, anyway.

Kittay flopped down near a sand dune and closed her moon- and lightning-reflected eyes. Amsterdam, who sat in the brush eating leaves, knew a cute couple when he sensed one. Panther wandered restlessly on the beach. That was cute according to Kittay. No one would argue. Don't mess with Panther---or, Kittay.

Benja snored on the turf behind Amsterdam.

There was Roberts, on the wet sand nearest the water. His eyes glowed, moon and lightning. He was exhausted, but he'd be ready to hunt again soon, whether it was day or night.

He needed to hunt smarter and forget these wave creatures.

It was night.

No doubt.

Thunder.

Panther growled.

"Shut up," said Butts.

"Go to sleep," said the big cat ... *smaller* big cat.

"Boys?" said Jamie.

"Quiet," said Emily.

"Ditto," said Chimp.

"I'm hungry," said Cindy.

"You gotta' worm," said Amsterdam.

"Shut up 'shuttin' up'," murmured Butts.

"I *hate* worms," said Cindy.

"*Shhhhhh*," said Rachel.

"Quiet!!" yelled Elaine, Brian, and Nathaniel.

"*Shhhhhhhh*," said Seysew.

"*Shhhhhhhh*," said Naja back at the clearing.

"Shut up 'shuttin' up,'" said Robert.

"*We are the champions, my frehhhhhhnnnd … doo doo … doo doo … doooooo wah diddy diddy dum diddy do*!!" sang the ant mass and pigeon horde.

"*You lost*!!" shouted the mass.

"*No.* You *did*!!" shouted the horde.

Back at the beach …

"I wonder," said a ready-to-slumber Amsterdam, "if you can hear those dudes in Key West?"

Snoring went on in earnest---different tones, timbres, strokes for different folks.

Another boom-boom from the latest looming squall.

"Doo wah diddy," murmured Peter, as he fell asleep on an oak branch on the outskirts of the clearing.

"What'd you say, boss?" said the first looey.

"Nothin'," said Boss Ant.

"O.K., boss," said the first looey.

"*Shhhhhh*," said the ant second looey.

"*Shhhhhh*," said the pigeon second looey.

William shifted his tail. He was laughing, probably dreaming, and farted, loud and long. Butts burped. So did Panther.

"You had to fart?" said Rachel.

"Everyone does," said Seysew.

They were spread out and supposed to be getting some shut-eye.

"Can I fart, too?" said Chipmunk.

"Shut up," said Kinle. The other lizards, also lounging on the beach, grunted on cue, reminding the others of those pains-in-the-ass ants and pigeons.

"*You* shut up!" That was Panther.

Benja farted.

"*Eeeuu*," said Jamie.

"Dude!" said Panther.

"It was my turn," said Benja. "Yes?"

END

365 | Douglas Walter

367 I Douglas Walter

369 I Douglas Walter

371 I Douglas Walter

373 | Douglas Walter

Made in the USA
Columbia, SC
15 March 2020